A HARD

BARGAIN

☆

"I'm not going to waste time asking you a hundred questions about the Blue River Gang—at least not right now. But if we get out of this, and it comes time for you to spill the beans about Ash Wheeler, you better hold up your end of the bargain," Torn said sternly.

"Or what?"

"Or I'll haul you right back to the Blue River Breaks and let Wheeler have you."

She stood there for a moment, looking him square in the eye.

"No you won't. In fact, you'll be in love with me before we get halfway to Broken Bow."

Torn laughed. "You have a high opinion of yourself, Miss Lane."

"Call me Chancey. And so do you, Clay, thinking you can get me out of here alive."

"It's Judge Torn to you," said Torn, turning away. "And I never said I thought I could get you out alive."

Also by Hank Edwards

THE JUDGE

WAR CLOUDS

GUN GLORY

TEXAS FEUD

STEEL JUSTICE

LAWLESS LAND

BAD BLOOD

RIVER RAID

BORDER WAR

DEATH WARRANT

IRON ROAD

Published by
HARPERPAPERBACKS

THE JUDGE

LADY
OUTLAW

Hank Edwards

HarperPaperbacks
A Division of HarperCollinsPublishers

This is a work of fiction. The characters, incidents, and dialogues are products of the author's imagination and are not to be construed as real. Any resemblance to actual events or persons, living or dead, is entirely coincidental.

HarperPaperbacks *A Division of* HarperCollins*Publishers*
10 East 53rd Street, New York, N.Y. 10022

Cover illustration by Tony Gabriel

First printing: April 1994

Printed in the United States of America

HarperPaperbacks and colophon are trademarks of HarperCollins*Publishers*

10 9 8 7 6 5 4 3 2 1

CHAPTER

1

HAD IT NOT BEEN FOR THE PAWNEE RENEGADES, CLAY Torn figured he would have made it to Lonesome Pine in time, maybe, to avoid the shootout with members of the Blue River Gang that resulted in the death of Sheriff Bill Logan. In which case he would probably have had a lot less trouble with the feisty outlaw, Chancey Lane.

But that was all hindsight, and nobody knew better than Torn how worthless hindsight was. Looking back, he would have done a lot of things differently. He wouldn't have become the frontier's most notorious federal judge, for one thing. In which case he would not have been running for his life across the Nebraska badlands with a passel of no-account Pawnee scalptakers howling on his heels.

No, he would have been back in South Carolina,

1

where he'd been born and raised, and where, at times like this, when hot lead burned the air around him, he knew with absolute certainty that he belonged. He would have married his fiancée, Melony Hancock, instead of going off to fight some foolish war, all decked out in Confederate gray, and he and Melony would have lived happily ever after, because she wouldn't have been abducted by Yankee deserters during his absence, and brought west, and he would not have spent the last dozen years of his life looking for her.

There were four of them.

Tribal outcasts. Scavengers of the plains. Diehards who refused to live on some reservation—if you could call that living. Gaunt and bloodthirsty, they survived by accosting anybody unlucky enough to cross their path.

They had come busting out of a ravine, blasting away, and until then Torn had been blissfully ignorant of their presence. He'd kicked his lanky claybank into a stretched-out gallop and bent low his lean frame to present less of a target.

And the race was on.

He had a .45 Colt Peacemaker in a holster on his hip and a Winchester repeating rifle in the scabbard tied onto his three-quarters rig, but he did not bother trying to bring either firearm into action. Trying to hit a target at a couple of hundred yards away from the back of a galloping horse was at best an exercise in futility and at worst a lamentable waste of ammunition. Instead, he concentrated on urging every iota of speed out of the claybank horse beneath him.

For a moment it seemed to be working—at least the renegades weren't gaining on him.

Then fate took a hand.

The claybank stepped into a gopher hole hidden in the sun-parched grass. The animal uttered a scream and went down. Torn whipped the Winchester from its scabbard and jumped clear. He hit the ground on his feet, but stumbled. He spun, working the Winchester's lever action. The claybank was on its side, thrashing. Without hesitation, Torn brought the rifle to his shoulder and fired, putting a bullet in the animal's brainpan.

He ran back to the horse, realizing he would have probably kept rifle cartridges in his saddlebags. The claybank had fallen on its left side, the ammunition was in the right-side pannier. Lucky. It was the little things like that which spelled the difference between life and death.

He shoved the box of 44/40 cartridges into a pocket of his dusty black frock coat. A quick glance told him the renegades were less than a hundred yards away now. They were still shooting up a storm. He stood there, almost disdainful in his stance. He'd been under fire countless times before, first as a Confederate cavalry commander, then as a federal judge who passed sentence on dozens of frontier hardcases.

He looked around. There was a ravine thirty yards behind him. That and the claybank's carcass was the only cover, and he opted for the ravine. All he needed to do was buy himself enough time to reach it.

Bringing the Winchester's stock to shoulder, he laid down a blistering fire in the direction of the renegades. He had the range down and the elevation calculated, and he didn't really try to pick specific targets. The hot summer sun glimmered off the brass of spent shell casings that jumped out of the rifle's receiver as he worked the lever action fast as he could.

One of the renegades somersaulted backward off his horse. The pony of another went down, nose-diving into the ground, hurling its rider through the air. The man got up slowly, reeling. The other two checked their horses, unnerved by this hail of bullets, and dismounted to conceal themselves—or try to—behind their fiddle-footed mounts. They held onto their reins with one hand and tried to use their thumb-busters with the other.

Now, thought Torn, was the time to make a run for it. The men shooting at him were standing on solid ground, so their marksmanship was bound to improve, and while the range was still a little long for accuracy with a short-gun, Torn decided to retreat.

He lit out for the ravine.

He was tall and lean, and his long legs consumed the distance in great galloping strides. He didn't look back. He didn't need to, to know that the renegades were trying to remount. That wasn't easy to do. Their horses were all worked up from the hard run and the guns going off all around them. By the time they were back in the saddle and girding their lathered ponies forward, Torn had reached the ravine. He skidded down to the bottom, moved to his left a dozen strides, and then clambered back up the steep bank. Loose dirt and rock gave way beneath him. He slid back, scraping his hands, banging his knee, and indulging in a sharp curse.

The Pawnees were still shooting at the spot where he had disappeared into the ravine. Torn crawled up to the rim and drew a bead. He fired once. The renegade he'd been shooting for reeled in the saddle, struck in the shoulder. Torn fired again. The Pawnee plunged to the ground, hit squarely in the chest by the second bullet. His riderless horse veered off and headed for places unknown.

The last two renegades spun their horses and galloped away.

Torn watched them go, daring to hope that they'd had their fill.

But the Pawnees pulled up, out of rifle range. Ground-hitching their horses, they split up, running crouched low, using the contours of the land to good advantage, and in no time at all had vanished completely from Torn's view.

Torn slid back down to the bottom of the ravine and checked the lay of the land. He needed a good defensive position because the two remaining renegades were stalking him.

CHAPTER

2

A FEW BENT-BOUGHED OLD SCRUB OAKS, THEIR LIMBS looking like groping skeletal fingers against the burnished afternoon sky, flagged the serpentine course of the ravine. They clung to the rim of the defile's steep banks. Flash-flooding had washed the earth away from their gnarled roots, which here and there jutted from the embankment.

It was at such a spot that Torn found a hideout. Here the embankment had been hollowed out behind the roots of one wind-swept tree. Rocks and deadwood carried by the raging waters of a flash flood or two had become lodged among the roots.

Torn took the precaution of probing into the cave with his Winchester. He didn't care to crawl into bed with a rattlesnake. Listening hard, he heard no rattling protest. Halfway satisfied that the cavity was unoccupied, he crawled in, squeezing his long frame between two big roots.

The cave was just big enough to accommodate him. It wasn't too comfortable, all scrunched up, but he got himself situated as best he could and checked the ravine through the flotsam-clogged roots. He could see a stone's throw in either direction. Good enough.

He settled back to wait. Patience had never been his long suit, but sometimes you had no choice but to exercise it. Especially out here on the frontier where great distances were involved, it sometimes seemed like you had to ride for a couple of forevers just to get from one lonesome town to the next, and where the trains seldom ran on time, or the stage coaches, either, and where sometimes, in some parts of the country, the game was scarce when you were starving, and the waterholes all dried up when you were dying of thirst.

There was no way of knowing how long the two renegades would take to close in.

Torn reckoned he would have to kill both of them. With most Indians, *discretion was the better part of valor.* If they couldn't get what they wanted with relative ease they usually backed down, believing it wiser to live to fight another day. But with these renegades it was altogether different. They had no tribal rules or customs to which they adhered. No home that they might want to live to see again. They were scavengers with nothing at all to live for except plunder and murder. They placed no value on human life, not even their own.

Minutes dragged by like hours.

It was only natural for Torn to wonder if he was a prayer away from dying. If he lost, the renegades would take his weapons and boots and clothes and leave his naked carcass for the *other* scavengers of the plains—the wolves and the buzzards. His bones would soon be picked clean and scattered, to bleach in the sun. And no one would likely ever find even those remains. People just disappeared out here in this big country, never to be heard from again. And in Torn's case, no one would shed a tear.

Bill Logan, the sheriff of Lonesome Pine, was expecting him, but Logan wouldn't lead a search party out to find him if he became long overdue. The Lonesome Pine badgetoter had enough trouble on his hands with Chancey Lane, the legendary lady outlaw.

They said Chancey Lane was the prettiest woman west of the Mississippi and east of the divide. The deadliest, too. For years she had ridden the owlhoot trail with the Blue River Gang, the most notorious bunch of *longriders* since the James brothers and their outfit. She had been Ash Wheeler's woman. Ash Wheeler was the leader of the Blue River Gang and the most wanted man on the frontier.

According to Logan, Chancey Lane had just ridden into Lonesome Pine and given herself up. She wanted protection from Ash Wheeler. Once she was safe, she promised to identify every member of the gang—and there were quite a few—and produce a map that would reveal the several hideouts used by the gang in the breaks of the Blue River. That happened to be the wildest, meanest country in Nebraska. Many a posse had gone in after the outlaws in the aftermath of a bank robbery or stage holdup. None had ever gotten far—least of all, far enough to stumble on one of the gang's hideouts. Most had limped out of the breaks, bloodied and broken.

Right now Chancey Lane was in the Lonesome Pine jail, guarded by Logan and a platoon of deputies. But she wouldn't talk. Said she wouldn't be safe until she was in Lincoln, hundreds of miles from Ash Wheeler's stomping grounds, and under the eagle-eyed protection of U.S. Marshals.

Logan had wired the state governor. The governor had wired the U.S. Attorney General. Now Clay Torn was on his way to Lonesome Pine to find out what Chancey Lane was up to. For his part, Sheriff Logan just wanted Chancey out of his hair. He'd had a lighted stick of dynamite tossed in his lap the day Chancey rode in, and he couldn't wait to pass it to someone else.

And he was expecting Clay Torn to be that someone else.

Torn *wanted* to get to Lonesome Pine. He wanted to use Chancey Lane to nab Ash Wheeler and his gang. Ash and his owlhoot hellions had been running roughshod over this territory for years, thumbing their noses at the law. Torn wanted a shot at them. Wanted it bad.

But first he had to get past these two renegades.

One of them had just crept into sight.

Torn's first inclination was to slide the barrel of his Winchester through the roots and plug the man.

He decided against it because he didn't know where the second man was, and until he knew it would be foolhardy, if not fatal, to give his position away.

So he waited.

CHAPTER 3

THE RENEGADE CREPT CLOSER, IN A HALF-CROUCH, RIFLE swinging this way and that, murder in his black eyes. He wore an old, ragged army tunic, leggings, and a battered derby hat. Squat, bow-legged and dirty, he was a scruffy looking character.

Torn didn't move and barely breathed, as the man came closer. The renegade saw that there was a cave behind the roots of the twisted tree. His black eyes narrowed as he tried to peer inside. But the sun was too bright, and the cavity where Torn was hiding too dark, for him to make anything out.

He'll see my boot prints in the sand, thought Torn, *when he gets a little closer.*

Where the hell was the other renegade?

Closer came the renegade. He scanned the rim of

the ravine, looked behind him, then up ahead, and at the cave again.

Then he glanced at the ground.

As Torn had expected, he saw the boot prints.

The renegade whirled, rifle at hip level.

He got off one shot. The bullet smacked into one of the thick, gnarled roots.

Torn slid the Winchester through the roots and fired once, twice. The renegade staggered backward. Torn's Winchester spoke again. The impact of the head shot picked the renegade off his feet and slammed him to the ground.

The last renegade was nowhere to be seen. Torn cursed under his breath. He knew the man was near —he could sense it. And he had given his position away. But he'd had no choice.

Question now was whether he stayed put and waited for the last renegade to come to him.

He decided to take the fight to his adversary. Why hide in this hole when he'd lost the element of surprise?

Crawling out from among the roots, he was straightening the kinks out of his back, checking both directions, when the renegade launched himself off the rim directly above the hole from which Torn had emerged.

The renegade let out a bloodcurdling scream. Torn spun around, but before he could bring the Winchester to bear, the renegade collided with him.

The impact knocked Torn down and knocked the wind out of him. He lost his grip on the Winchester which fell to the ground. The renegade had a pistol in hand; he pointed it at Torn's head. Torn knocked it aside just as it discharged. He felt gunpowder burn his cheek. The gunshot rang in his ear, deafening. The bullet plowed into the sand.

Torn drove a rock-hard fist into the renegade's face. Blood spewed from the man's nose. The blow knocked him backward, and Torn squirmed out from under, jumped to his feet, reached for his Colt Peacemaker. The renegade was still on the ground. He fired at Torn. The bullet went wide. Torn drew and fired with the speed of a rattler's strike. The bullet slammed into the renegade's chest. But he was a tough customer. He tried to bring the pistol up again. It had suddenly grown very heavy. Torn took two steps closer, raised his gun arm, elbow locked, and took careful aim. He knew these men gave no quarter, and expected none. Merciless, his gray eyes bleak, he squeezed the Peacemaker's trigger.

The bullet entered the renegade's left eye and blew the back of his head off. His body flopped in the sand. His boot heels drummed briefly. Then he lay still forever.

Torn drew a deep breath and holstered the Colt. Retrieving the Winchester, he climbed out of the ravine. He noticed the lone buzzard circling high overhead.

Looking for the horses of the renegades, he saw one, a couple hundred yards away, ground-hitched. Torn started toward the cayuse. When he got close the horse eyed him balefully. The reins were secured to a rock the size of a man's head. Torn moved closer still. The horse reared, front hooves flailing. The reins snapped, and the cayuse crowhopped away.

With another softspoken curse, Torn scanned the high plains for the three other horses. They were nowhere to be found. Just his luck. Resigned to the fact that he had a long walk ahead of him, Torn returned to the carcass of his own horse. He left the ten-dollar saddle, taking only the saddlebags and canteen. The saddlebags contained his few belongings: razor and hand-mirror, a bar of lye soap, an extra shirt, and—most importantly—a bundle of letters Melony had written him fifteen years ago, when he'd been in Virginia fighting Yankees with Lee and Jackson and J.E.B. Stuart, and she'd been home in South Carolina, waiting for him to come back to her. Those letters—and the faded daguerreotype of her, which he carried in the pocket of his frock coat, were all he had in the way of mementos.

Draping the saddlebags over his shoulder, Torn turned his steps west. Lonesome Pine was a good day's walk away. Sheriff Logan would just have to wait a little longer to get shed of Chancey Lane.

C H A P T E R

4

THE RENDEZVOUS SITE WAS A COUPLE MILES OUT OF LONE-some Pine, up along Dog Leg Creek, which really wasn't a creek at all, but rather a bone-dry wash full of sand and stone.

The three men who rode out of Lonesome Pine that night were all owlhoots. One was Big Jack Eades, a bearded codger with a glass eye and a sour expression. He favored a sawed-off shotgun and carried it in a shoulder strap so that all he had to do was swing it up under his right arm and aim in the general direction of whatever he was shooting at. Generally, with a sawed-off, that was all you had to do.

He hadn't been carrying the scattergun in Lonesome Pine the past few days, because it just didn't fit into the role he'd been playing—that of a horse trader. In fact, he'd missed his old ten-gauge and kept touching it fondly as he rode. He liked to load it with a mixed blend of deadly projectiles: horseshoe nails, small sharp rocks, anything he could think of to augment the double-ought.

His son rode with him that night. Johnny Eades was every bit as mean and nasty as his father. Like father, like son, or so they said, and the two generations of Eadeses who rode along Dog Leg Creek that night were living proof.

Johnny Eades was a little better looking than his father. Not much, but he fancied himself a lady-killer, nonetheless. Women were his weakness. He also hankered after easy money, all of which he spent on sporting ladies. The easy money he liked most was the kind that came out of safes and strongboxes.

Until fairly recently both father and son had been engaged in rustling. It was the only vocation Big Jack had known, prior to falling in with Ash Wheeler and the Blue River Gang. He had raised his sons to follow in his crooked footprints. One had ended up dancing on the end of a rancher's rope. It was then that Big Jack had decided to try his hand at train robbery and stage holdups.

The third rider was named Lucky Jones. His first name was really Lucifer. They called him Lucky because, like a cat, he seemed to have been blessed with nine lives. As a youngster he'd been a slave on the sugarcane plantation of a Louisiana man who had a sadistic streak a mile wide. One day Lucky had stolen a little food for his ailing mother. He'd been apprehended and sentenced to a hundred lashes. A hundred stripes would have killed a lot of men. Somehow Lucky had survived. The lesson he had learned was how to hate.

Later, during the war, he'd run off and joined the Union, enlisting in one of the Negro regiments, and been shot in his first engagement. The army surgeon had pronounced him as good as dead. But Lucky Jones had recovered fully.

After the war he had drifted west, tried his hand as a cowboy and freighter. Comanches had "killed" him once—or so they had thought. Since taking to the outlaw trail he'd been "killed" twice more.

Johnny Eades had passed himself off as an out-of-work cowboy while in Lonesome Pine. He was pretty good with a deck of pasteboards, so he played cards in the saloons and won a little money, which he spent on the painted women, and kept his ears open, because you could learn just about everything worth knowing about a town in its watering holes. For that same reason Lucky Jones had gotten a job as a swamper in a bucket-of-blood saloon that just happened to be across the street from the jailhouse.

The three of them were going now to report on what they had observed the past two days in Lonesome Pine. Ash Wheeler was waiting for them. He'd hand-picked them for the job, because it was unlikely anyone in Lonesome Pine would recognize them. There was nothing more than vague general descriptions on the wanted posters out on Big Jack and Johnny Eades. As for Lucky Jones, there *was* a drawing of him on his current "paper." A damned good one. Thing was, most white folk had a hard time distinguishing one black man from another. Lucky's color was his best disguise.

The rendezvous site was a burned out homesteader's cabin. All that remained was the stone chimney and some charred timbers. The moon was up and three-quarters full, so there was plenty of light for a pack of sharp-eyed longriders to see by, and they could discern Ash Wheeler's lean form tilted up against the chimney stones as they rode up. The orange tip of a roll-your-own glowed in the gloom as Wheeler took one last drag. Then he flicked the quirly away and stepped through the blackened, weed overgrown ruins to greet them.

"What's the verdict?" he drawled.

No one spoke right off.

Ash Wheeler was a handsome devil of a man, broad in the shoulder, lean at the hips, with longish black hair and keen blue eyes and a becoming, at times boyish, grin. He wore a Remington Army model revolver on his hip and a Porterhouse .38 in a shoulder harness beneath his longcoat.

He was grinning now. A bright, amiable, infectious grin. But none of the other outlaws grinned back. None of them were put at ease. They knew how deceptive that grin of Wheeler's could be. You never knew what Wheeler was thinking, or what he was about to do. He was the most dangerous man any of them had ever met, precisely for that reason.

"Must be bad news," said Wheeler. "Don't worry. I know better than to shoot the messenger. Good or bad, news is what I sent you boys into Lonesome Pine for. You are my eyes and ears. I'd go in myself, except everybody and their grandmother knows my face, and most of 'em have seen it right above that part about the five-thousand dollar reward."

"Don't look good," admitted Big Jack. "That jailhouse is one tough nut to crack. Foot-thick adobe walls, so she won't burn."

"Well, Big Jack, we wouldn't want to burn Chancey up anyway, now would we?"

"Sheriff Logan's got himself six deputies. At least three are on duty all the time. The rest eat and sleep right there. Only one's let out to go about the town at a time. I'm told the jail's a damned arsenal."

Wheeler pursed his lips. "So we can't take it by storm. What about from the inside?"

Big Jack shrugged. "Maybe."

"Maybe? Well, maybe one of you had better get yourself arrested."

"They're not putting anybody else in there," said Johnny. "A couple of drunks just got tossed out of town."

"Yeah," grumbled Big Jack. "Talk is, if a feller was to shoot somebody, they'd just string him up from the rafters of the livery barn 'fore they stuck him in jail where Chancey's being held. Logan ain't taking no chances."

Wheeler rubbed his chin. He looked up at the moon.

"Then we'll just have to wait, I reckon."

"For what?" rasped Lucky Jones. He didn't relish having to spend even one more day in the role of saloon swamper. The clientele didn't pay him no respect. And when one of them talked down to him it was all he could do to keep from filling the sonuvabitch full of lead.

"We'll wait," said Wheeler, "for them to bring Chancey out."

CHAPTER 5

"WHEN'LL THAT BE?" ASKED LUCKY, DISGRUNTLED.

"They say Logan wired the federal boys," said Johnny. "He wants Chancey off his hands."

Wheeler chuckled. " 'Course he does. 'Cause he's afraid of me. Afraid of what I'll do to him. And to the entire town of Lonesome Pine, if he hurts one hair on her head."

"What will you do?" asked Johnny, with a crooked grin.

Wheeler's expression was a stony mask. "There won't be no more Lonesome Pine, Nebraska," he replied coldly.

"That kinda sounds like fun," said Big Jack, his one good eye twinkling.

"I've heard a federal judge is on his way," said

Johnny. "You hear a lot hangin' around in a saloon all day."

"You spend most of your time in some whore's bed," said Lucky.

Johnny laughed. "Whores talk, too. Fact is, men tell them sportin' ladies things they'd never tell their wives. So, if you treat the ladies nice, you can find out a whole lot about what's goin' on in a town."

"That's what I call undercover work," chuckled Big Jack.

"Who is this judge?" asked Wheeler.

"Man called Clay Torn."

Wheeler's eyes narrowed. He nodded. "Yeah. I've heard of him. A man who'll walk 'on down."

"Ain't he the one who shut down Hadley Fourcade's bunch over in Missouri?" asked Lucky.

"Yeah. And Jack Jenkins and his bunch of river pirates."

"Well, he ain't tangled with the Blue River Gang yet," said Johnny.

"So what's he coming to Lonesome Pine for?" asked Wheeler. He wasn't really asking, just wondering out loud. "To take Chancey off Sheriff Logan's hands?"

"What else?" asked Big Jack.

"To talk things over with her," suggested Johnny.

"What things?" snapped Wheeler.

Johnny cast an anxious sidelong glance at Big Jack.

"What would Chancey have to talk over with the likes of Clay Torn?" pressed Wheeler.

Johnny gulped down the lump in his throat. "I'll tell you what I heard, Ash. Just remember what you said about shootin' the messenger."

Wheeler's infectious smile flashed again. "Don't fret."

"Well," said Johnny, hesitant, not completely convinced by that smile. "Talk around town is that Chancey turned herself in."

"That's a dirty lie." Wheeler's smile was frozen.

"They say she's promisin' to tell ever'thing she knows about you and the rest of us. Who we are, where our hideouts are down in the breaks. All that. In return for protection."

Wheeler's smile had vanished altogether. "Protection from what?"

"From you."

Wheeler took a step forward. There was menace in that step. Johnny braced himself. So did Big Jack. Johnny figured it was his daddy's scattergun that prevented Ash Wheeler from beating him to a bloody pulp. Big Jack was prepared to die for his boy. It was probably Big Jack's only redeeming virtue.

With a glance at Big Jack—and Big Jack's sawed-off double-barrel—Wheeler decided to stay put. He even managed to force a grin. But it was strained. So was his voice.

"That's pure-dee horse puckey," he said. "Chancey loves me. She knows I'd never hurt her."

Big Jack almost made a derisive sound. But he caught himself. No need to push Wheeler over the edge. The man was mad-dog crazy. One of the few men Big Jack had ever been afraid of.

He knew Chancey Lane was afraid of Ash Wheeler, too. And with good reason, in Big Jack's studied opinion.

Because Wheeler was a jealous sort. He imagined that Chancey was flirting with just about every hombre in the Blue River Gang. He perceived Chancey to be a woman of easy virtue and loose morals.

Big Jack didn't share that perception. Sure, Chancey Lane talked a little rough and acted somewhat brazen at times. But Big Jack had a hunch most of that was just for show.

Wheeler didn't. He suspected Chancey of jumping into the sack with every man who came down the pike. And when he got good and drunk, sometimes, Wheeler hit her. He'd start yelling at her, making accusations, and Chancey would give back as good as she got, because the one thing Chancey Lane wouldn't do was stand there meek as a lamb and take any abuse.

So Big Jack figured it was entirely likely Chancey Lane was afraid of Wheeler. Not that he was too happy with Chancey for running to the law—if indeed that was what she had done—but he could sure see how it could happen.

"Okay," said Wheeler. "This is what you'll do. Go back to Lonesome Pine and wait for this federal judge to show up. I reckon Sheriff Logan will prevail upon him to take Chancey as far away as he can. Which won't be far. Because when Chancey steps out of that jail you'll be there. And if you have to go through some federal judge to get to her, fine."

"Just the three of us?" asked Johnny.

"Can't the three of you take on one man?"

"There's Logan's deputies, remember?"

"Yeah. I remember. I'll send in a few more of the boys."

"If Torn takes her we could wait until they rode out of Lonesome Pine," suggested Big Jack.

"No," snapped Wheeler. "I want her as soon as she comes out of that crossbar hotel. You hear me, Eades? I don't care who gets killed—I want her back."

CHAPTER

6

IT WAS AFTER DARK WHEN TORN TRUDGED SURE-FOOTED
into Lonesome Pine. He wanted a bath and a shave
and a decent meal and a soft bed to stretch his tired
frame out on, and he wanted those things a lot worse
right then than he wanted to see Chancey Lane. But
he had a job to do, so he compromised and settled for
getting the first three and postponing the fourth,
much as he hated to.

He checked into the first hotel he came to—for all
he knew it was the only hostelry in Lonesome Pine.
Acquiring a room, he left his saddlebags there, spared
the four-poster bed a longing glance, and then went
next door to the barber shop. This establishment had
a couple of footed cast-iron tubs in a rear room, sepa-
rated by a pair of blankets hanging from a rod. Torn
had a shave while the bath water was being heated in

big kettles over a firepit out back. Then he luxuriated
in a hot bath for the better part of a half hour.

While there his clothes were sponged and brushed.
Clean and clean-shaven, and feeling human for the
first time in days, Torn ventured down-street to a res-
taurant. He ate a big dinner—steak and potatoes
washed down with good strong java.

Only then did he proceed to the Lonesome Pine
jailhouse.

He noticed thick wooden shutters with criss-
crossed gunslots on the tall, narrow windows. The
timbered door was reinforced with sharp iron. His
knock on the door elicited an immediate response—
the barrel of a shotgun protruded from the gunslots in
one pair of shutters.

"State your name and business," growled the man
on the other end of the ten-gauge.

"Clay Torn. Federal judge."

"Can you prove it?"

"No, I can't. So I reckon I'll go back where I came
from. Be sure to tell Sheriff Logan I stopped by."

He turned to go.

Then he heard a bolt thrown. The door creaked
open and a pot-bellied, gray-haired man exploded out
onto the boardwalk.

"Judge Torn? You're Judge Torn?"

The man shot anxious looks up and down the
street.

"Come on in, then. I've been expectin' you."

Torn followed the man inside. He noted the ball-
pointed star on the man's shirt, figured this was Logan. The sheriff hastily slammed the heavy door shut
and slid the bolt home. Torn took a quick look
around.

There were two other men in the room. One sat behind a desk, his feet propped up. A rifle lay across the desk. He was tossing pasteboards into an upside-down hat—and missing almost all the time, because he was watching Torn like a hawk. The other man stood near the window. He'd been the one with the shotgun. The shotgun hung down at his side now. But he was facing Torn, and the shotgun could swing up into action in a split second. Torn knew it would, too, if he made one wrong move.

There was tension in the air—and behind the eyes of Logan and his two deputies. Torn didn't wonder. By the cluttered look of the office—dirty pans on the White Oak stove, soogans rolled out on the floor, clothes here and there. These local starpackers had been forted up for some time.

"Glad you're here," said Logan, with vast relief. "And don't take offense, but I'll be gladder when you leave. 'Cause that means Chancey Lane will be leavin', too. How many marshals did you bring along with you?"

"None."

"None?" Logan's jaw dropped.

"And I didn't come to take Chancey Lane anywhere. I was sent here to talk to her."

"Talk to her?" echoed Logan, chagrined. Then he frowned. A heartbeat later he was wearing a crimson scowl. "Now look here, Judge. I want that hellcat out of my jail, you hear? I got a responsibility to the folks hereabouts. My constituents. Long as Chancey's here, everybody in Lonesome Pine is in danger."

"From Ash Wheeler?"

"That's right. He's plumb loco."

"Crazy enough to take on a whole town?"

"Damn right."

"How many men ride with him?"

Logan shrugged. "Twenty. Thirty. Nobody knows for sure. Enough to raise hell. I'm surprised they ain't come chargin' in here, them gallop-and-gunshot boys, shootin' up everything and trying to bust her out."

"Wouldn't be easy, busting her out of here."

"Point is, I've done my share. You're here now, so you take over. I'm finished with Chancey Lane, as of tonight."

Torn's anger was on the rise. He was on the verge of telling Logan that he was a local who would obey federal authority—in other words, that he would do what he was told.

But he didn't.

"You scared of Ash Wheeler, Sheriff?"

Logan's face turned a deeper shade of crimson. "Watch your mouth, Judge."

Torn's smile was smooth and only half-friendly. He realized as he got older he grew less tolerant of cowards and blowhards.

"Just wondered," he drawled. "You act spooked. Surely, when you ran for sheriff, you knew you'd cross paths with bad hombres every now and then."

"It's the railroads and stagecoaches that have a bone to pick with the Blue River Gang. It's them and the federal government, on account of them owlhoots tamperin' with the mails, that put up the rewards. Wheeler and his hellions ain't never done nothing to Lonesome Pine, and Lonesome Pine's my bailiwick. You go out and ask the folks of this town if they're pleased to have Chancey Lane as their guest. You won't find five who say other than to get her out of here."

"So you're just an elected official doing what his local constituents want him to do." Torn shook his head, reached out, and tapped the badge on Logan's shirt. "You're forgetting one thing. When you put on that star you swore to uphold the law. You work for the law, Sheriff."

"You better take Chancey Lane out," said Logan darkly. "If you don't I might just throw her out."

Torn stared. "If she's telling the truth, you'd be signing her death warrant. Wheeler would kill her for trying to turn him in. That would be cold-blooded murder, Logan."

"I'm just telling you," snapped the truculent star-packer. "She goes, one way or the other."

Torn was silent a moment. He realized Logan would be of no help whatsoever. No point in trying to exercise federal authority here.

"Okay," he said. "Let me see her."

CHAPTER 7

LOGAN LED HIM INTO THE CELLBLOCK.

Another deputy sat in a chair in a passageway flanked on either side by two strap-iron cells. There was a door, barred, at the far end of the passageway—Torn figured it led out back. The deputy had a shotgun across his lap. There was a small, scarred table pushed up to the door of one of the cells. Two arms were extended through the iron of the cell door as the prisoner shuffled a deck of cards.

"Chancey," said Logan, "here's someone to see you."

"Hell," said Chancey Lane. "I was fixing to win the keys to this place."

Logan fired a sharp look at the deputy.

"Christ, Sheriff, she's just kidding," said the deputy. "Tell him you're kidding, Chancey, for Pete's sake."

Chancey laughed, a throaty laugh. "We're just passing the time, Sheriff, playing a little blackjack."

"Get out of here, Luke," said Logan.

The deputy beat a hasty retreat to the office. Torn and Logan moved on down the passageway and Torn got his first look at Chancey Lane.

She was attractive, which surprised Torn. Though she wore male garb, and her sun-burnished complexion was not the honey and cream one would expect of an eastern lady, there was no mistaking her for anything besides a woman. She was slender, of average height. Her face was a little too long, her mouth a little too small, and her nose too sharply bladed, but these were minor imperfections. Her curly auburn hair was short, hacked off just below the ears. Sultry eyes—big, gold-flecked hazel eyes—were her best feature.

Chancey gave Torn a brazen once-over.

"You a federal marshal?"

"No. Federal judge."

"Most of the judges I've seen are fat and bald."

"Seen a lot of judges, Miss Lane?"

Her smile was lopsided. "I've been hauled up before a few, yeah. Now you—you look more like a gunslinger. You got a hideout under that coat."

"Sharp eyes," said Torn, "but it's not a pistol."

He opened his coat so she could see the saber-knife in its shoulder harness. Her eyes widened.

"Wait a minute. I think I've heard of you. Can't recall the name, but I've heard tell of a judge who carries a pigsticker like that."

"Clay Torn."

"You've come to deal?"

"I've come to take you out of here."

"Well, I got to admit, I'm getting pretty tired of the

accommodations. No offense, Sheriff. How many men riding with you Judge?"

"How many do you think I need?"

"What's the cavalry doing?"

Torn smiled. "It's just me, Miss Lane. I'm all they sent."

"Maybe I'll just stay here a while longer," she glanced at Logan. "But then maybe again I won't."

"What are you scared of?" asked Torn.

"Ash Wheeler. And so would you be, if you weren't too dumb to know better."

"Okay, maybe you have a right to be scared. But if you do everything I tell you to do, when I tell you to do it, you just might make it through."

She gave him a snappy salute.

"One thing," said Torn, sternly. "I'm not going to waste time asking you a hundred questions about the Blue River Gang—at least not right now. But if we get out of this, and it comes time for you to spill the beans about Ash Wheeler and his gang, you better hold up your end of the bargain."

"Or what?"

"Or I'll haul you right back to the Blue River Breaks and let Wheeler have you."

She stood there a moment, grasping the strap-iron of the cell door with both hands, and looked him square in the eye.

"No you won't."

"Don't be too sure."

"Oh I'm sure. In fact, you'll be in love with me before we get halfway to Broken Bow."

Torn laughed. "You have a high opinion of yourself, Miss Lane."

"Call me Chancey. And so do you, Clay, thinking you can get me out of here alive."

"It's Judge Torn to you," said Torn, turning away, "and I never said I thought I could get you out alive."

CHAPTER

8

BACK IN THE OFFICE, WITH THE DEPUTY NAMED LUKE back at his post and the door to the cellblock closed, Logan couldn't wait to ask Torn when he was leaving.

"I'll need two horses first," he replied, a little cross.

"What happened to yours?"

"Pawnee renegades, a day east of here."

"Lucky they didn't get you."

"You mean lucky for you, or me?"

"I mean lucky for Chancey Lane," snapped Logan.

"Well, luck had nothing to do with it. Where can I get a couple of horses?"

"I'll give you a couple of horses, if that's what it takes to get her out of here."

"Right generous of you, Sheriff," said Torn, sardonic. "I'll write you out a requisition and you can collect on it from the federal government."

"I said I'd donate the damned cayuses. When are you riding out?"

"First light. Think you can hold out that long?"

Logan's eyes narrowed. "We'll manage."

Torn gave a curt nod, threw the bolt in the front door and stepped out into the night without another word spoken.

From the hotel a hundred yards east of the jail and across the street, Big Jack and Johnny Eades, along with a half-breed Mexican *pistolero* named Valdez, watched Torn angling across the darkened street from the window of a second-story room.

"That's him," said Johnny. "That's the man the clerk downstairs told me signed in as Clay Torn."

Valdez and Big Jack took their first long look at Torn. The former was one of the three that Ash Wheeler had sent in to Lonesome Pine as reinforcements for Big Jack, Johnny, and Lucky Jones.

"Tall-walkin' sonuvabitch," murmured Big Jack.

"Wonder what will he do?" asked Valdez, stroking his mustache, his black eyes a-glimmer.

"Reckon he'll take Chancey out," said Johnny. "Way I hear it, Logan would insist on it."

"I hope so," said Big Jack. "I don't much care for this whole business. Chancey Lane is nothin' but trouble, and I ain't sure that the same can't be said for Ash Wheeler." He cast a sidelong glance at Valdez. " 'Course that's between the three of us."

"*Que?*"

"Don't act all innocent, Valdez. You cain't pull it off. I mean what I said about Wheeler stays in this room. If he finds out I said it, I'll blow a hole in you big nuff to see next Christmas through. Savvy?"

"Si," said Valdez. He harbored profound respect for Big Jack and his sawed-off shotgun.

"What do we do now?" asked Johnny.

"Wait," said Big Jack. "Just like we been doing."

"I can't wait to try that federal judge on for size."

"Sometimes I wonder if you come from my loins, boy. You ain't got the sense God gave a sage hen."

"Way Ash told it, that pilgrim's some kind of legend," said Johnny. "He don't look so special to me. Besides, there's six of us, and only one of him."

"I ain't too proud to work with six-to-one odds," said Big Jack, "and I ain't dumb enough to think about glory. I just wish we could wait until Torn takes Chancey out of town before we move in."

"We can't," reminded Johnny. "Ash said he wants her freed as soon as she walks out of that jail."

"I know what he said," barked Big Jack. "And I'll do it. But that don't mean I have to like it." He sighed. "Valdez, go find Finney and Calder and Lucky Jones and fetch 'em here. Reckon we best get our plan built, seein' as how it's likely Torn'll be riding out with Chancey tomorrow. I'll want ever'body in place at dawn."

Valdez left to do Big Jack's bidding.

"I like the idea of snatchin' Chancey away right here in the middle of town," smiled Johnny Eades. "In front of God and everybody."

Big Jack just grunted. "Just remember, we want Chancey alive. She gets kilt, I don't reckon our lives would be worth a bucket of spit."

"Relax Pa," said Johnny, in high spirits. "She won't get hurt. But I wouldn't want to say the same for Judge Clay Torn."

* * *

The sun, not yet risen, had colored the eastern sky a rosy pink when Torn rode up to the front of the Lonesome Pine jailhouse. Torn was riding a lanky dun horse and leading a blazed sorrel. One of Logan's deputies had dropped by his hotel room last night to inform him that the sheriff had arranged to have the mounts saddled and ready at the livery just down the street from the hostelry. Torn had looked them over and pronounced them satisfactory. He hadn't really expected Logan to palm off a couple of nags on him. Not as bad as the badgetoter wanted Chancey Lane out of his bailiwick. In fact, Logan probably would have presented him with a couple of racehorses, had any thoroughbreds been available.

His first stop that morning had been the telegraph office. He'd sent a wire off to Lincoln, which since 1867 had been Nebraska's capitol, and the site of a U.S. Marshal's office, requesting the dispatch of at least a couple of federal law officers to Broken Bow. Broken Bow was about halfway between Lincoln and Lonesome Pine.

Torn had slept well. He didn't much care for his prospects in terms of getting Chancey safely to Broken Bow, but he never let that kind of thing interfere with his sleep. Whatever happened, happened. Losing sleep over tomorrow was a waste of time. He'd learned that much in the late, unlamented war. A lot of soldiers had spent a lot of sleepless nights on the eve of the battle. Torn hadn't been one of them.

You just took one day at a time. No matter what came your way. If it was to your liking you accepted it, if not, you killed it.

He didn't even get a chance to dismount. No sooner was he in front of the jailhouse than the door swung open and Logan and one of his deputies—one Torn hadn't met last night—emerged with Chancey Lane between them.

"Here she is," said Logan. He looked as happy as a prospector who's just found the mother lode. "I'm turning the prisoner over to you, Judge. She's in your custody. Happy trails."

"You can't fool me, Sheriff," said Chancey. "You hate to see me go. You miss me already."

"Yeah. I'll miss you about as much as I miss my first wife, which is none at all."

"Where's the horse I rode in on?" asked Chancey, eyeing the blazed sorrel.

"That horse was stole. It had a Bar Ought brand on it. I returned it to its rightful owner. Count your blessings, lady. You could've had your neck stretched for horse-stealing."

"Somehow I wasn't worried."

"The sooner we go, the sooner we'll get there," said Torn.

"Aren't you gonna tie her hands, or something?" asked Logan.

"What for?"

"Give her those reins, Judge, and she might run out on you."

Torn's smile was chilly. "If she wants to run I'll let her."

"No," said Chancey. "I'm going with you, Clay."

"That's Judge Torn to you."

"Not that I figure we'll get very far."

"Get up on your horse, Miss Lane."

Chancey stepped forward, got both hands on the saddlehorn and swung, lithe as a cat, into the saddle. Torn handed her the reins.

Then, without a word to Logan, he kicked his horse into motion.

Chancey fell in behind him.

They didn't get twenty paces from the jailhouse before all hell broke loose.

CHAPTER 9

THEY CAME FROM ALL SIDES.

In front, Valdez stepped out of an alley on one side of the street. The outlaw named Finney, square-built and red-haired, wearing a long duster, emerged from a passageway across from Valdez. They had their short-guns drawn.

Torn checked his horse so sharply that the animal reared up on its hind legs.

That was the reason the man named Calder missed his long shot.

Calder was supposedly quite a hand with the rifle. That was why Big Jack had positioned him in the window of Johnny's second-floor room at the hotel down the street from the jailhouse.

The plan had been for Calder to fire as soon as Valdez and Finney appeared. The theory was that he'd have an unobstructed shot at Torn. Then Valdez and Finney would close in on Chancey Lane and grab her.

Meanwhile, Johnny and Big Jack came out of hiding behind Torn and Chancey. Their job was to deal with the sheriff and his deputies if they tried to interfere.

But Calder missed Torn clearly, which derailed Big Jack's entire plan.

Torn heard the gunshot, recognized it as a rifle, and knew the general direction from whence it came. He swung his horse around and kicked it into a lunging gallop. As he drew abreast of Chancey he came out of the saddle and swept her from hers. He tried to cushion her fall. The sorrel bolted. As Torn got back up on his horse, he drew the Colt Peacemaker.

Valdez was shooting now. A heartbeat later, Finney joined in.

Torn blazed away with the Colt. He didn't fan the hammer, thumbing it back each time, taking careful fire. In a gunfight, steady nerves and hands, and accuracy, were more important than speed.

Finney was struck in the chest by two of the three bullets Torn sent his way. The impact knocked the outlaw backward, sprawling. Torn had already swung toward Valdez, stepping sideways as he fired. He'd learned that in close-quarters gunplay it was best not to make yourself a stationary target.

Valdez knew this, too. Torn's first bullet missed. The second just winged the *pistolero*. Valdez jumped behind the nearest cover, a water trough.

Up in the hotel window, Calder fired again.

The bullet kicked up dust at Torn's feet. Torn had fired three times at Finney, twice at Valdez—he spent his last bullet shooting at the window. This time he'd seen the muzzle flash from the corner of his eye. A quick glance had located the window from which the rifle barrel protruded. He knew the range was long for short-gun accuracy—but it was worth the bullet if he got close and made the rifleman duck or, at the very least, flinch.

He got closer than he had a right to expect. The bullet splintered the window frame and Calder did duck back into the room, unnerved.

"Get up!" yelled Torn.

He reached down and grabbed Chancey's arm, dragged her to her feet, not even giving her time to obey his curt command. Then he angled for the jail-house. For the first time he saw Johnny and Big Jack Eades coming up the street.

Sheriff Logan and his deputy were about to enter the jailhouse when the shooting started. It didn't take either one of them long to understand what was happening. Logan's mood swung from positive euphoria to absolute consternation in a heartbeat. For one brief, ecstatic moment he had thought himself rid of Chancey Lane forever. He'd been congratulating himself for being one lucky so-and-so. He hadn't dared hope to get shed of the lady outlaw without some trouble from the Blue River Gang.

Obviously he'd been congratulating himself a little prematurely.

Watching Torn shoot it out with two of the long-riders, Logan had been reluctant to deal himself into the fray. He even caught himself considering a most unworthy option: letting Torn slug it out with the Blue River Gang. Just turning his back. So he hesitated.

The hesitation proved fatal.

Big Jack's scattergun boomed. The elder Eades was skulking up the street on the jailhouse side, and at first, neither Logan nor his deputy realized he was coming up on their blind sides. But when the two barrels full of horseshoe nails and pebbles and double-ought hit Logan the lawman found out quick.

Of course, Logan only had a few seconds to ponder the knowledge. That deadly mix blasting out of Big Jack's sawed-off opened him up. The impact slammed him backward into the deputy. Both men went down in a heap on the blood-splattered boardwalk fronting the jailhouse.

Logan lay there trying to breathe. But he couldn't. He stared at the sky, just now getting light. It was mighty cold for summer in the Nebraska badlands. That was his last thought. Then the sky turned black and he was gone.

The deputy squirmed out from underneath Logan. He was all in a panic. The sheriff's blood was all over him. He got off one hasty shot that didn't come anywhere close to either Big Jack or Johnny. Then Johnny's sixshooter spoke, and the deputy bounced off the front wall of the jailhouse and fell over Logan's corpse, a corpse himself.

His pistol, flung from a dead hand, landed in the street.

Torn scooped it up on his way to the jailhouse door.

He figured that if he could just get himself and Chancey behind those foot-thick adobe walls they would stand a fair-to-middling chance.

But then another deputy appeared in the doorway.

Torn recognized him. It was Luke, Chancey's card game partner.

Luke took one look at Logan and the just-killed deputy. He turned completely white. Johnny Eades took a shot at him. The bullet thudded into the adobe inches away from Luke, who promptly lost whatever nerve he had and jumped back inside the jail. He slammed the door shut and threw the heavy iron bolt.

CHAPTER 10

TORN MUTTERED A BITTER CURSE.

He and Chancey were almost to the door. Almost to safety. But now Luke had locked them out. There was a very good chance that by so doing he had signed their death warrants.

Torn slung more lead in the direction of Big Jack Eades and his son. He saw Big Jack's scattergun swing his way. Pulling Chancey down with him, he sprawled on the boardwalk behind the bodies of Logan and his deputy, the one piled on top of the other.

Big Jack's shotgun roared. Some of the load pelted the adobe wall behind Torn. Some of it struck the corpses behind which Torn and Chancey had taken shelter. None of it hit Torn.

"You all right?" he asked the lady outlaw.

"I'd feel better with a shooting iron in my hand."

She started to crawl over the dead men, reaching for the six-gun still in the deputy's holster.

Johnny Eades was waiting for a target. He fired. But Torn was quicker, pulling Chancey back down.

"Are you tired of living?" he asked, exasperated.

She didn't respond. At least, thought Torn, he had found out two things about her. She had guts, and she wasn't squeamish.

"Come on," he said. "We can't stay here."

Big Jack and Johnny were coming on.

He noticed Big Jack was still reloading the scattergun. So when Torn came up shooting, it was Johnny Eades he was shooting at.

As he stood, blasting away, he jerked Chancey to her feet.

"Stop yanking on me!" she yelled.

"Run!" He gave her a push in the direction he wanted to go, sent two more bullets Johnny's way, and turned to follow her.

Johnny Eades stumbled, dropped to his knees, clutching his bullet-torn midsection. The pistol slipped out of his grasp.

Big Jack stopped dead in his tracks and stared at his son. An incoherent sound escaped his lips. Johnny slowly lifted his head and stared at his father. His eyes were scared. He tried to speak, but no words came.

Then he pitched forward on his face.

Big Jack let out a roar that sounded like a wounded grizzly's.

Torn heard it, but he didn't look back. Chancey was running along the boardwalk fronting the building adjacent to the Lonesome Pine jail. It was a clapboard structure housing a general store.

Across the street, Valdez was emerging from behind the water trough.

With long loping strides Torn caught up with Chancey. Valdez started shooting. A bullet plunked into the front wall of the she-bang. Another slapped into an upright. Torn hooked an arm around Chancey and plunged straight through the store's plate-glass windows.

There were a couple of barrels standing just inside the windows. Torn and Chancey fell over them, landed in a rain of glass shards. Crackers spilled out of one barrel and potatoes out of the other. Picking himself up, Torn sent a bullet through the broken window and watched Valdez dive back behind the water trough.

It was his last bullet and he knew it. A quick glance around the store located the boxes of ammunition on a back shelf. He grabbed one, turned to see that Chancey was sitting in the crackers and potatoes, picking glass fragments out of her short auburn hair.

"Would you mind getting up, Miss Lane?"

She smirked and got up.

"How about a gun, Clay?"

"No."

"I'm a good shot. I can help."

"I'll manage."

"You'll manage . . . to get us both killed."

"We're not dead yet."

"The day is young."

"Let's go."

He headed for the back door, opened it just a crack, and peeked out.

At the back corner of the building, a black man was

standing with several saddled horses, reins in his hands.

Lucky Jones was looking down the alley between the general store and the next building, toward the street where Valdez and Big Jack were converging on the front of the mercantile.

According to Big Jack's plan, Valdez and Finney were supposed to grab Chancey and bring her down the alley. Then all of them would mount up and dust out of town, to rendezvous with Big Jack, Johnny, and Calder.

Lucky Jones couldn't see much of anything. All he could hear was some shooting. He didn't like standing around, but out of respect for Big Jack's scattergun he was going to do what the elder Eades had instructed him to do.

Since all the action seemed to be taking place on the street, Lucky's attention never strayed from the alley. As a result, Torn was able to slip up on him from behind.

Torn hadn't taken the time to open the box of cartridges and load his pistol. He had two empty six-guns, and that wasn't too smart in the middle of a gunfight, but the only reason he and Chancey were still alive was because they had kept on the move. So he belted the empty revolver that had once belonged to Logan's deputy—the Colt Peacemaker was back in its holster.

Then he reached under his frock coat.

The saber-knife was strapped to his side, snug against his rib cage, upside-down in a custom made shoulder-rig. All he had to do was slip a rawhide thong off the hilt and the weapon slipped out of its sheath and fell into his waiting hand.

He gestured for Chancey to linger in the doorway, then cat-footed up on the unsuspecting Lucky Jones.

One of the horses Lucky Jones was holding gave him away with a snort and a jerk of its head.

The outlaw whirled. Torn closed in and drove the saber-knife into the man's midsection. With his free hand, he wrenched the reins out of Lucky's grasp. Lucky Jones went down. Torn withdrew the saber-knife. The outlaw curled up in a ball, clutching his ripped-open belly.

"Come along, Miss Lane," said Torn as he climbed into the saddle of one of the three horses.

Chancey vaulted aboard one of the others. Torn let the third go.

They rode out of Lonesome Pine.

CHAPTER

11

THEY DIDN'T STOP UNTIL SUNDOWN, EXCEPT TO LET THEIR horses breathe with cinches loosened, and drink a little water poured out of a canteen into the crown of Torn's hat. A couple of times they walked for a spell. Having ridden with J.E.B. Stuart—the consummate cavalryman—during the war, Torn knew how to get the most out of a mount in a day's time.

Scarcely a word passed between them all day. Torn was lost in his own thoughts, brooding over the killings that had occurred in Lonesome Pine that morning. He thought it was too bad that Sheriff Logan and his deputy had lost their lives. It wasn't that he'd much cared for the sheriff, but he still considered it a shame.

He figured that Ash Wheeler had sent his gang into Lonesome Pine to kill Chancey Lane, and he shared this opinion with her as they sat around a small fire down in a hollow with the night closing in around them.

Chancey disagreed. "Ash sent those boys in to take me alive."

"You're saying Wheeler would take you back, knowing you'd tried to make a deal with the law at his expense?"

She wore a funny, crooked smile. "He'd want to give me a kiss before he put a bullet in me."

Torn's eyes narrowed. If what Chancey said was true, then Ash Wheeler was a crazy, cold-blooded hombre. But he made no comment.

He'd found a can of beans in one of the saddlebags; now he opened the can with his saber-knife. Chancey stared at the unique weapon.

"Don't worry," said Torn, "I cleaned the blade off."

"Where did you get it?"

"Long time ago." Torn's voice was bleak. "I spent some time in a prisoner-of-war camp during the war. Point Lookout. There was a sergeant-of-the-guard there. Man named Karl Schmidt. This used to be his saber. When I escaped, I took it away from him."

"You killed him?"

"Yeah. It was the least I could do to pay him back for all the times he had me flogged and beaten. Later, the blade broke. I honed it down to what you see now. Carried it ever since."

"Why?"

"It's quiet."

So was Chancey, for a moment. Finally, she said, "You didn't give Lucky Jones a chance."

"No. I don't play fair. That's why I'm still alive."

"You don't mind killing." It was an observation.

"Yes, I do mind it," said Torn. "But I'd mind getting killed a lot more. You sound disapproving, Miss Lane. And that surprises me. After all, you've ridden with outlaws. I wouldn't think you'd have a lot of scruples left."

"You're judging me by the company I keep."

"That's what happens."

He'd found a spoon in the saddlebags, too. Once the beans were hot, he handed both spoon and can to Chancey. She ate a little, gave it back.

"Did you know all those men back there?"

She nodded. "All the ones I saw. The Mexican's called Valdez. The one with the scattergun is Big Jack Eades. I think you killed his son, Johnny Eades. Which means Big Jack will track you down if it takes until hell freezes over. You'll have to kill him, or look over your shoulder for the rest of your life."

"Who else?"

"Finney. You curled his toes, too. I don't know who it was in the hotel, with the rifle. And then Lucky Jones. I wonder if Lucky's dead."

"What do you mean?"

"He's hard to kill. That's why they call him Lucky."

"Who else rides with Wheeler?"

"Oh no, you don't. That's all you're getting out of me about the Blue River Gang until you get me to Lincoln. If I told you everything I knew then you wouldn't need me anymore. This way, you've got a stake in keeping me alive."

"Don't you trust me, Miss Lane?"

She laughed. "Nothing personal, but I don't trust anybody."

"Maybe you'd see your way clear to telling me what you figure they'll do next. Big Jack Eades—will he come after us straightaway, or report back to Wheeler?"

"Oh, he'll run off to Ash. And then Ash will round up every owlhoot in the Blue River breaks and track us down."

"And how many men, exactly, would that be?"

"More than you can handle."

"You don't give much for our chances."

Chancey shrugged, gazed pensively off into the night shadows. "I never expect anything out of life."

"How did you fall in with Ash Wheeler?"

For a moment she did not answer. Just kept staring off into the night, as though she hadn't even heard him. But he knew she had. He just wasn't sure if she would open up to him. So he waited.

"Indians killed my folks when I was just a kid," she said, finally, her voice husky. "My only other kin were my grandfolks on my mother's side. They lived on a little farm just north of Cairo, Illinois. They worked me like I was some kind of slave. Treated me worse than they'd treat a slave. Well, I got enough of that real quick, as you might imagine. So I kept my eyes open for a way out.

"The way out was a Yankee peddler named Faraday. I was fifteen when his wagon rolled up to the house. Well, almost fifteen. When he rolled away the next day, I was with him." She glanced at Torn. "Want all the gory details, Judge? He was about forty years old. Drank too much rye whisky. He took me along 'cause I made him feel good. I would've slept with the Devil himself to get away from that place."

"Did I say anything?"

"No, but you were thinking it."

Torn shrugged. He wasn't about to argue the point.

"I put up with fat-gut Faraday about as far as Independence, Missouri. Then I slipped away from him and fell in love with a gambler name of William Wright. He was a lot nicer to me than that peddler was. He didn't force his attentions on me. You could say he was a real gentleman. Always polite around me. Saw to it that I was well-fed and well-dressed. Taught me a few tricks of his trade. I got pretty handy with the 'California prayer book.' Pretty handy, too, with a gun. Wright taught me how to shoot. He said I had a dead-eye talent."

"What happened to him?"

She shook her head. "Same thing that happens to a lot of card sharks. Some drunken cowpoke lost all his money, figured Wright was bottom-dealing, and shot him dead. Wright wasn't a cheat. I'm sure of that. When I heard the news I slipped into Wright's hotel room—we never shared a room, since you were wondering—because I knew he kept a box full of cash in his trunk. He called it his "grubstake." It was several hundred dollars. I took it. Maybe I didn't have any right to it. But he didn't have anybody else to leave it to. If I hadn't taken it, somebody else would've. The hotel clerk, or the sheriff. Somebody. So I took it. Bought a fifty-dollar horse and a twelve-dollar saddle and lit a shuck.

"I didn't know where I was going. California, I think. I'm not sure if I really cared. Well, I never made it to California. Got about this far and fell in with Ash Wheeler.

"I thought I was in love with him. He's a handsome devil, I'll give him that much, and smooth talking. Being a kid of seventeen—almost seventeen—I guess I was still pretty naive. I thought he loved me, too. And

I thought the outlaw life was . . . glamorous. I think that's the word?"

Torn nodded. "That's the word. But not the right word for the life of an outlaw."

"I found that out. I also found out that Ash Wheeler didn't really love me. He loved *owning* me. Same way he loved owning a new horse, or a brand new repeating rifle, or a shiny pair of spurs. Ash likes to *own* things. And once he owns them, God help anybody who tries to take them away. It didn't take me long to realize I was trapped. Ash Wheeler wasn't the type to let me go just 'cause I asked. Fact is, when I talked about leaving, he beat me.

"I admit it—I was afraid of him. So I stopped thinking about leaving. Tried to make the best of a bad situation. Stuck it out for more than two years."

"What changed your mind?"

"A boy named Wiley Tucker. He was a nice boy. A little wild. My age or maybe a little younger. He signed on with the Blue River Gang. I liked Wiley. Wiley liked me.

"There was nothing going on between us. We were just friends. We hit it off right away. But Ash didn't believe that. He's real jealous, Ash is. So one day he picked a fight with Wiley and shot him dead. He prodded Wiley into drawing down on him, but it was cold-blooded murder.

"Right then I decided to get away, no matter what. And I made up my mind that Ash Wheeler was going to pay for killing Wiley. So I watched for my chance. One day, when Ash was off scouting a bank—if you get me to Lincoln I'll tell you which bank in what town —I rode off to Lonesome Pine."

Chancey was quiet for a while, gazing into the fire.

"That's it. That's my life story. Not much to brag about, huh?"

She rolled up in her blanket and was soon fast asleep.

Torn killed the fire. He sat up for a spell, thinking about all she had told him and listening to the night.

Eventually he, too, went to sleep.

CHAPTER 12

THAT DAY BIG JACK, VALDEZ, AND CALDER RODE OUT TO meet Ash Wheeler at the ruins of the homesteader's cabin on Dog Leg Creek.

This time Wheeler didn't wait for them to come to him. He walked out to meet them, his strides long and angry. It was obvious something was wrong—he could see that Chancey wasn't with them. That infuriated him. When things didn't go his way he got mad. But he struggled to keep his temper in check. He needed to get some details.

"What happened?" he asked, his voice hard as steel.

"My son is dead," said Big Jack.

Wheeler's eyes narrowed as he studied Big Jack's face. Big Jack's expression was inscrutable. Wheeler watched him the way a man would watch a dog that was rabid. If Big Jack got pushed too far, in his present state of mind . . . well, that scattergun could do big damage in very little time. This realization helped Wheeler calm down. A sawed off ten-gauge could do that.

"I'm sorry to hear it," he said. "Truly sorry. How did it happen?"

Big Jack glared across at Calder. They, and Valdez, were still mounted, stirrup-to-stirrup. The Mexican *pistolero* was in the middle. Calder was mighty glad of that.

"For one thing, Calder missed his long shot."

Big Jack's tone of voice was downright lethal—the comment sounded like a death sentence to Calder.

"Torn's horse reared just as I fired," he said by way of defense.

"Then Valdez here, and Finney, took Torn on," said Big Jack. "Johnny and me come up from the other end of the street. Finney got kilt. As you can see, Ash, Valdez got winged."

"Is nothing," said Valdez. A bloody bandanna was tied around his arm—a makeshift dressing. It was all Valdez would do for himself, apart from partaking of some ninety-proof liquid medicine when he came across some. Torn's bullet had just grazed him, cutting a deep furrow in his flesh.

"Sounds like a lot of lead was flying," said Wheeler. "Somebody tell me Chancey's okay."

"She's okay," said Calder.

"Did Torn kill your son, Big Jack?"

Big Jack Eades simply nodded.

"What about Logan and his deputies? Did they deal themselves in?"

"Logan and one of his deputies are dead," said Big Jack.

"What a shame," said Wheeler. He wasn't sincere. "Where's Lucky Jones?"

"That judge cut him open," said Big Jack. "Lucky was holdin' some of our horses. We were gonna grab Chancey as soon as she got out of that jail and make a quick getaway. That's the way you wanted it, Ash, so that's how we aimed to do it. But Torn got to Lucky and cut him bad, then he and Chancey rode off, on our cayuses."

"Lucky's dead?"

"Well, he wasn't quite dead when we left. We couldn't hang around and wait for him to die, either. And we couldn't bring him along. I figure the Lonesome Pine sawbones will try to stitch him back together, if there's a chance for him. But he would've died for sure had we thrown him across a horse and tried to bring him out." Big Jack shrugged. Even on a good day he wouldn't have cared if Lucky Jones lived or died.

Ash Wheeler didn't care, either. He wasn't concerned about the loss of Lucky Jones, or Finney, or even Johnny Eades. Longriders who would jump at the chance to join up with the Blue River Gang were a dime a dozen. He'd have no problem replacing three dead.

And he wasn't worried about Lucky talking to the law if he survived. The man knew better. Knew that if he talked about the Blue River Gang he would die. That was a guaranteed fact. So Lucky would keep his mouth shut and do his time, or even dance on the end of a rope—depending on the sentence—without betraying Wheeler and the others.

"Okay," said Wheeler, thinking fast. "I reckon Torn

headed east. Toward Broken Bow. Maybe Lincoln. He can find help there."

"What kind of help?" asked Calder.

"U.S. Marshal help. Big Jack, you and Valdez head back to the breaks. Round up everybody. Bring 'em to Hinckley's Ferry. I'll meet up with you there."

"I ain't goin' back to the breaks," was Big Jack's flat response.

Wheeler just looked at him. He didn't like back talk. He expected the men who rode with him to jump when he told them to jump. But considering Big Jack's frame of mind, he stepped cautiously.

"Then where you reckon you're going?" he asked quietly.

"I'm gonna pick up Torn's trail. I'm gonna track that bastard down. Then I'm gonna make him pay for killin' Johnny. I came here to tell you what happened. That's all. I have a score to settle with that judge, and I won't be kept from it."

Wheeler nodded. "Okay, Big Jack. You do what you have to do. Valdez, it's up to you to get the rest of the boys to Hinckley's Ferry. You savvy?"

"Si, Ash. You can depend on me."

"Yeah."

"What do I do, boss?" asked Calder.

"You'll ride with me. We're gonna head on up to Scottsville. Get a telegraph off."

"A telegraph? To who?"

Wheeler smiled. "Not all badgetoters are my enemies, boys. I've got one or two who owe me a favor."

"How's that?"

"Ain't none of your business."

"Sorry, Ash."

"Fact is, there's a one-horse town called Reddon

Springs twixt here an Broken Bow. And there's a two-bit lawdog there who'll do what I tell him to do if he doesn't want to host a necktie party. I reckon if Torn passes through Reddon Springs he'll get a big surprise."

"Torn won't make it that far," said Big Jack.

"I hope you're right," replied Wheeler pleasantly. "Just remember one thing, I want Chancey back without a scratch on her."

"Oh, I'll bring her back," promised Big Jack. "And I'll bring you Judge Torn's head, while I'm at it."

CHAPTER 13

"WE'LL NEVER MAKE IT, YOU KNOW."

She said it matter-of-factly, right out of the blue, as they were riding across the monotonous, sun-burnt prairie their second day out of Lonesome Pine.

"You don't give a man much of a chance to prove himself," said Torn.

"Oh, you don't have anything to prove, Clay."

"Look, Miss Lane, I keep telling you . . ."

"I know you're one tough hombre. They wouldn't have sent you down here all by yourself if you weren't."

"Bringing you back wasn't my job."

"And the way you handled yourself back there in Lonesome Pine." She shook her head. "I've been around some hardcases in my time, Clay. . . . Sorry,

I mean Judge. I've never seen anybody so . . . so calm and collected under fire."

"Doesn't do much good to panic," said Torn. "I tried that the first time I saw action in the war."

"You were in the war?"

Torn nodded. He didn't really care to dig up old memories.

"Which side?"

"The losing side."

She was silent a moment. "You'd be surprised how often you can cheat death and get away with it."

"But you don't think we'll make it."

"I know Ash Wheeler. He'll stop at nothing to keep me from reaching Lincoln."

"Men who'll stop at nothing can still be stopped."

She didn't respond to that.

Coming to a creek—a shallow trickle of water through a bed of rocks and shaded by a few scrawny trees, Torn decided it would be a good place to spend the night. It was a little early to stop; they had an hour of daylight left. But he hadn't seen a sign of pursuit in two days, and was beginning to think there wouldn't be any. Maybe Chancey was wrong. Maybe Ash Wheeler wouldn't round up every owlhoot in the Blue River Breaks and come after them. It was possible that the Blue River Gang had concluded the jig was up; perhaps they were even now splitting up and heading for the tall timber, resigned to the fact that Chancey Lane had gotten away and was going to talk to the law.

Maybe.

Fact remained, their horses were tired, so an early stop would benefit them. It was hot, and here was shade. They were thirsty, and here was water.

And that gave Chancey Lane an idea.

"Are you a gentleman, Judge?"

"I used to be."

"Well, reason I ask, I'd like to get cleaned up, if you know what I mean."

Torn glanced at the creek. "Reckon there's enough water in there for a bath, do you?"

"I'll manage, thank you."

"I promise not to look, Miss Lane."

She gave him a sidelong coquettish look.

"Not even peek?"

"No," he said sternly. Dismounting, he unsaddled his horse and paid her no more attention.

A trifle hurt, Chancey headed down to the creek. She unbuttoned her shirt. A glance at Torn over beneath the trees revealed that he was busy building a small fire, his back to her. She sighed, disappointed, and removed her shirt. Sitting on her heels, she splashed herself with water. Another glance in Torn's direction. His back was still to her. So she slung the shirt over her shoulder and strolled along the creek a ways until she found a pool where the water was a foot or more deep. Sitting on a rock, she pulled off her boots. Sat there a while, soaking her feet, enjoying the warmth of the setting sun on her bare back.

Why, she wondered, was Torn's apparent indifference to her charms of any consequence to her? She *did* find him attractive. But why would he want to have anything to do with a woman like her? He was, after all, a federal judge. Mister law-and-order. Probably had a wife and kids somewhere. Probably went to Sunday service, when he wasn't out rounding up bad men. An upright citizen. And who was she? A lady outlaw—and the "lady" part didn't fit.

But it was a shame, mused Chancey, that nothing, obviously, would happen between her and Torn. A little tenderness—a bit of affection—would be nice, considering the fact that they were both going to die any day now.

Chancey was convinced of that. Somehow she just knew she'd never see Lincoln. Or even Broken Bow, for that matter. Ash was going to kill her. That was why she'd run out on him in the first place. Not so much on account of what he'd done to that poor boy, Wiley Tucker. But because she'd come, finally, to the realization that it was just a matter of time before Ash Wheeler killed her, in a raging fit of blind jealousy. The man was crazy.

She should have known there was really no escape. Not from a man like Ash Wheeler. Her only chance would have been to kill him first. Put a knife between his ribs while he slept. She saw her mistake now. She should never have left the Blue River Breaks while Ash still breathed.

Problem was, she couldn't have done it. She just didn't have it in her. As bad as she was, she wasn't that bad.

She shrugged, then smiled to herself. She'd made her bed. Now she'd have to lie in it.

It was just too bad that she couldn't lie in it with that hardcase federal judge yonder. Now there was a hell of a man.

She stood up, shed her pants, and thought about how long it had been since she'd worn an honest-to-God dress. Maybe if she wore a pretty dress and some of that war paint like the calico queens wore, then Torn would pay her some attention. But who was she fooling? The man had sharp eyes. He would see right through all that get-up—see her for what she was.

Her eyes suddenly burned with hot tears. She bent down, cupped water in her hands, and washed the tears off her cheeks.

"You're an empty-headed fool, Chancey Lane," she said, scolding herself.

She heard a footstep behind her. Heart leaping into her throat, she grabbed for her shirt and whirled, expecting—hoping—to see Torn there, and blushed furiously, which amazed her, because she hadn't blushed for so long, since that first time with the Yankee peddler.

But it wasn't Torn standing there.

It was a big, burly man wearing a star, with a Henry repeater racked in his shoulder, standing hipshot and grinning at her.

"You might be empty-headed, ma'am," he said gruffly, "I couldn't say. But the rest of you is filled out just fine."

CHAPTER 14

"**WHO THE HELL DO YOU THINK YOU ARE,**" SNAPPED Chancey, too infuriated to be scared, "sneaking up on a lady like that, damn it!"

The man held up a hand, chuckling. "Whoa! I wasn't sneaking up . . ."

"The hell you weren't," said Chancey, her eyes spitting fire.

"Lady, huh? Don't know about that. You talk like a mule-skinner."

"Who are you?"

The man thumbed the star pinned to his leather vest. "The law. Sheriff Ben Rawlins, from Reddon Springs."

"That badge suppose to make me feel safe?"

Rawlins grinned. "Where's your saddle pard, ma'am? I seen your camp. Two horses."

Chancey's eyes got wide. She looked beyond Rawlins. She could see the trees beneath which Torn had made their camp. A wisp of blue smoke curled up from a small fire. Yes, there were the horses, each on a long tether.

But where was Torn?

Suddenly Chancey was apprehensive.

She didn't like the way the sheriff's eyes kept flicking across her body. It didn't matter if he was a lawman or not. He was still a man. With a man's desires. And she was out here stark naked and, to make matters worse, unarmed.

Where in God's name was Torn?

"I . . ." She didn't know what to say. Or what to do. "I . . ."

Rawlins shook his head. "Just who are you, lady? And what are you doing way out here in this big lonesome? You should never stray this far from camp without a gun, I'll tell you that much. There's a lot of bad hombres out here on this godforsaken prairie. Outlaws and Pawnee renegades and the likes. You're just lucky it was me and not one of them."

"Yeah," said Chancey. "Real lucky."

"I asked you a question," said Rawlins. "I want to know who you are."

"Go to hell."

Rawlins took a step toward her.

The bullet ricocheted off a rock between them and went screaming away. The rifle's report shimmied on the still, hot air. Chancey jumped. So did Rawlins. They both looked around and saw Torn standing on a cutbank fifty feet away, silhouetted against the blood-red dying sun.

Torn had the rifle to his shoulder. He worked the

lever action. An empty shell casing went spinning, winking in the crimson sunlight.

"Where are your manners, Sheriff?" asked Torn.

Rawlins' gun hand moved closer to the pistol in his holster.

"I'd hate to have to kill you," said Torn. "I'm a federal judge. That's all I'm going to say."

"That's all you need to say," said Rawlins. "We're on the same side."

"Then why don't you move your hand away from that charcoal-burner?"

Rawlins held his arms out away from his body. "Ease off, friend."

Torn lowered the rifle. He jumped down into the creek bed and walked over.

"Where were you?" snapped Chancey, furious.

"I heard him coming," said Torn.

"You left me out here as bait," she said, getting madder by the second.

Torn didn't bother responding. "Sheriff, if you've got a pot, I've got some coffee."

"It's a deal," said Rawlins. He glanced at Chancey, touched the brim of his hat. "Sorry I interrupted your bath, ma'am."

"Oh, I bet."

The two men turned and headed back for camp.

Fuming, Chancey got dressed and followed them.

"Reddon Springs is just a few miles east of here," said Rawlins. "Reckon you could've made it today if you'd pushed on."

"Didn't know," said Torn. He sipped his cup of crank. They all sat on their saddles around the small, crackling fire. Night had fallen. Off in the trees, a hoot

owl queried the darkness. One of the horses whickered softly.

"You say you're a federal judge," said Rawlins. "This
your circuit?"

"Not usually."

"Then what brings you out this way?"

"I . . ."

"More java?" Chancey jumped up, grabbed the cof-
feepot balanced on the stones rimming the fire, using
a bandanna to keep from burning her hand on the
handle.

"Thanks, darlin'," drawled Rawlins, as she topped
off his tin cup. "What were you saying, Judge?"

"I . . . *ouch!*"

Chancey had splashed coffee on his hand. Torn
jumped up, dropping his cup.

"I'm so sorry!" gasped Chancey.

Her back was to Rawlins. She looked Torn straight
in the eye and mouthed the word *don't*.

Torn said, "Don't worry about it."

"You could use a little axle grease to slap on that
burn," remarked Rawlins.

"It's not bad." Torn sat back down.

Chancey picked up his cup. "Would you like more
coffee?"

"No thanks," said Torn wryly. "I've had enough."

"So what brings you out here, Judge?" asked Rawlins again.

"It's federal business," replied Torn. "Don't take it
personal, Sheriff."

"Aw hell, I don't." chuckled Rawlins.

"What about you?" asked Torn. "You looking for
somebody?"

"What?"

"On somebody's trail?"

"There's been cattle rustled around here of late. Just checking with some of the ranchers. Lucky I just happened across you two. You wouldn't mind sharing your camp tonight, would you?"

"Reckon not."

Rawlins nodded. He put down his cup, stood and flexed the kinks out of his back, a rueful expression on his face. "Hate to say it, but I'm beginning to feel my age. Use to, I could ride from can-see to can't-see and then do-si-do the night away with the dance-hall girls. But I guess I'm getting long in the tooth. Fact is, I'm tuckered out. So, I think I'll just turn in."

As Rawlins unrolled his blankets, Torn glanced at Chancey. She shook her head, hesitant to say anything in Rawlins' presence.

Torn grimaced. Wondered what the hell was going on. He knew now that Chancey had staged the "accident" with the coffee to prevent him from telling Rawlins who they were and what they were doing. But why? The man was a badgetoter. So what was the problem?

One of the horse whickered again.

"I think I'll check the horses," said Torn, making it sound casual.

He stood up.

Chancey said, "I'll go with you."

"I don't think so," said Rawlins.

He turned, pistol in hand.

Torn figured it was Chancey that Rawlins was about to shoot. He didn't know why. It made no sense. But there was no time to think. He grabbed Chancey and threw her down and reached for the Colt in his holster

—knowing all along that he didn't have a chance, but knowing, too, that he had to at least try.

Rawlins' gun spoke and spat flame.

An explosion of pain, a blinding flash of white, and then Torn's world turned black, and he was cartwheeling down into the blackness, down, down, down . . .

CHAPTER

15

THE FIRST TIME TORN CAME TO HE WAS LYING ON STONY ground, looking up through the treetops at a sky half-dark. His head felt like someone had split it open with a dull ax. He reached up to touch his temple. A cloth, wet with blood, had been wrapped around his head.

His mind was quite clear. He had been shot, suffered a head wound. It was serious. By some miracle he was still alive. But maybe not for long. He felt very cold and numb, as though all the life had left his body.

"Clay . . ."

Who was that? A woman's voice. He could barely make it out. Sounded like whoever was calling him was a million miles away.

He thought about Melony. His blood-stained hand inched across his chest. He felt the shape of the daguerreotype in the pocket of his frock coat, over his heart.

Then he passed out.

The second time he came to he was lying in the back of a springboard wagon being bounced and jostled down what had to be the worst excuse for a road in the country. There was a blanket doubled up under him and another rolled up under his head. But they didn't help much. Every violent jerk of the wagon made his head hurt, an excruciating pain. Torn figured if someone stuck a red-hot iron through his eye and into the middle of his skull it wouldn't hurt as bad as this. He couldn't even see straight, for the pain.

Then he felt a cool touch—someone's hand on his cheek, and he looked over and saw Chancey Lane sitting beside him.

"Mister, his eyes are open!" she exclaimed.

"Well," came a gruff, laconic voice, "reckon that means he's still above snakes, don't it?"

At that moment a wagon wheel dropped down into a hole and bounced out again, and Torn was lifted bodily off the bed of the wagon. When he landed his head was cushioned by the rolled blanket, but that didn't make any difference.

He blacked out.

When he came to the third time he was lying in a bed, on a good feather mattress that felt like heaven. A crisp sheet and a quilt covered him to the chin. A woman stood at a small table next to the bed, dipping a cloth in water contained in an enamel bowl, wringing it out. She was an elderly woman, her iron-gray hair pulled back in a stern bun. In spite of her advanced years, she was slender and straight. Her face was sun-dark and deeply lined. It was a kind face.

Torn could tell by the face that this woman had endured many hardships, yet hadn't lost her compassion or good humor. She wore a plain gingham dress, mended in places, a little frayed at collar and cuffs.

"Who are you?" he asked, and his voice was surprisingly strong and clear.

She jumped at the sound of it.

"My word," she gasped. "You gave me a start."

"Sorry."

"How do you feel?"

"Like I'd have to get better to die."

She smiled. "You won't die, young man."

"Where am I?" Torn looked around, trying not to move his head. The room was small but handsome in a homey way.

"I'm Eliza Burkhart. My husband Malvern and I— this is our home."

"How did I get here? Where's . . ."

"She's safe and sound. Don't worry. You're a lucky man, to have such a brave wife."

"What?"

"Your wife, Abigail. She's a very brave young woman."

"Abigail?"

But Eliza was already to the door. She opened it, called out, "Malvern! Abigail! He's conscious."

Chancey rushed in.

"Oh, darling," she said, grasping his hand in both of hers. "Thank heavens."

A man entered the room to stand just inside the door. He was old, with a creased, leathery face and squinty, sun-faded eyes. But his step was limber, if a little horse-warped. He wore overalls, the legs tucked into mule-ear boots, a shirt with the sleeves rolled up.

"Well," he drawled, "good thing I ain't a bettin' man, Liza. 'Cause I woulda bet the homestead this pilgrim was gonna cross the river 'fore nightfall."

Torn recognized the gruff voice from his brief moment of consciousness in the wagon.

"Malvern Burkhart," scolded Eliza. "What a truly awful thing to say."

"I didn't mean nothin' by it," grumbled Malvern, on the defensive.

"You old coot," said Eliza fondly. "Come on. Let's give these two young people a little privacy."

They left the room, shutting the door behind them.

"Abigail?" asked Torn coldly.

"What was I supposed to do?" whispered Chancey. "Tell them who I was? Don't you think they'd know the name Chancey Lane? I couldn't take any chances. I had to get you some help, and I wasn't sure if they would help a notorious outlaw like Chancey Lane. So I'm Abigail. That was my mother's name."

"I guess I can buy that," said Torn reluctantly. "But what about the wife part?"

"It was the best way I could come up with explaining what we were doing together."

Torn figured the best place to start was at the beginning.

"Okay, what happened? Where's Rawlins?"

"Dead."

"Dead? How?"

Chancey was impassive. "I killed him."

"You?"

"I picked up your gun and shot him."

"He just stood there and let you do it?"

"He told me to drop the gun. Oh, he was going to shoot me. But he didn't want to. I figure his orders were to take me alive. He knew if he killed me, Ash Wheeler would hunt him down and kill him. That was guaranteed. Before he could decide which way to go, I shot him."

"Wheeler? What's Wheeler got to do with Rawlins?"

"I remembered Ash talking about how he owned some two-bit lawman. That's Ash—it's always who or what he owns. I never heard a name. But Ash said this lawman was beholden to him. Seems Ash wanted to steal a gold shipment, but he didn't know which stage it was coming through on. This lawman found out for him. In return, he got a share of the loot."

"I'll be damned. So if that was Rawlins, I can see how Wheeler thought he had him in his pocket—if Wheeler had proof he could produce."

"All he'd need to do is convince Rawlins that he did. And that couldn't have been too hard. That big galoot wasn't too smart."

"He outsmarted me," said Torn ruefully.

"The badge had you fooled."

"But how did you know that it was Rawlins?"

"I didn't," replied Chancey with a shrug. "But then, I don't trust coincidence."

"I see what you mean . . . Abigail." Torn smiled. "I reckon you saved my life. Rawlins would've put another one in me once he saw I was still breathing."

Chancey looked ashamed. "I ran out on you. Got on one of the horses bareback and lit a shuck. Didn't get far though, before I changed my mind and rode back. Because I knew you were still alive. Didn't know for how long. God, your face was covered with blood. It didn't look good. But I wrapped a bandanna around it to try and stop the bleeding."

"How did you find the Burkharts?"

"When I took off, I saw a road. We weren't but a mile from it. After sitting there all night, wondering if every time you drew breath would be the last time, I went back to that road at first light. Mr. Burkhart came along in a wagon. Said he was headed for Reddon Springs to pick up some supplies. I was lucky."

"*I* was lucky," said Torn. "How did you explain Rawlins?"

"I told him the sheriff had happened along and shared our camp with us. Just like Rawlins told it. That sometime in the night renegades had bushwhacked us. They killed Rawlins and almost killed you. But the two of you had put up a fight and run them off. Malvern was too worried about you to check around for sign. He believed me straight off. So we brought you here. It was closer than town, and Malvern seemed to think you'd fare just as well here, and have a better chance of recovery, than if he hauled you all the way to Reddon Springs and left you to the mercy of the local sawbones. I think the way Malvern described the doctor there was 'drunken butcher.' Judge, I lied to them about us because I wanted to get you some help." Again she looked away. "They're nice folks. And they like me. I . . . I don't think they would if they knew who I really was."

"There's one problem with that," said Torn. "Looks like you were right about Wheeler. He'll stop at nothing to get you back. Which means we have the whole Blue River Gang on our trail. And our trail leads here. Is it fair to put the Burkharts in danger like that? They ought to at least know what's coming."

She nodded. "You're right. I'll tell them."

She started for the door.

"Chancey."

She turned, a look of surprise on her face.

"No more 'Miss Lane,' Judge?"

"Call me Clay. And *we'll* tell them. After all, you and I are in this together."

CHAPTER 16

IT WAS AN EXERCISE IN WILLPOWER THAT GOT TORN OUT of bed that day, but he managed, at least as far as the next room. There he sank gratefully into one of the ladderback chairs around the table, which formed the room's centerpiece. Over there was the fireplace, with two good chairs around it and a handsome fowling piece above the mantel. Over here was the kitchen, where Eliza hovered over a pot of stew and another of coffee, cooking on the stove. The place had a clean, comfortable, lived-in feel to it.

"You have a nice place here," said Torn.

"Been here for more'n thirty years," said Malvern. "Put in a lot of sweat and blood. Reckon we'll die here. Hell, we were here long before there was a Reddon Springs."

"Malvern Burkhart," scolded Eliza. "Watch your language in front of our guests."

"Yes, Ma." He winked at Torn, with a sly grin, and Torn could tell he wasn't really browbeaten. Nor was Eliza really a scold. This was a game they played.

"We look after ourselves," said Malvern. "Always have. Some people say we're getting a little long in the tooth to stay way out here. Eliza's friends in town tell her we ought to move to Reddon Springs. But I don't feel a day over fifty. Way I see it, counting years is a waste of time. You're as young as you feel. Ain't nothing we did twenty years ago that we can't still do." He grinned with playful lechery at his wife. Eliza grimaced and shook her head, like a teacher who has come to realize, sadly, that all her efforts have been wasted on a recalcitrant student.

"We built this place ourselves," Malvern went on. "For awhile we was set up as a way station for a stage line but it went belly-up. Then I did some freighting of my own. Now mostly, I hunt and fish. I . . ."

"Malvern," said Eliza, coming over to pour them some coffee, "you're rambling. Excuse him, folks. He doesn't get too much company out here. When he does he tends to talk their ears off. Mister, you don't look too well. Maybe you shouldn't be up and about like this."

"I'm not much for bed rest."

Eliza sat down with her own cup of coffee and smiled at Chancey. "I hope you don't think I'm forward for saying this, dear, but you remind me so much of our daughter. When she was younger, of course."

Malvern gave Eliza a sharp look. Chancey looked startled.

"Really? Thank you. Where is she?"

It was Eliza's turn to give Malvern a strange look—but Malvern was squinting out the window. Eliza glanced down at her hands and shrugged.

"She married a cattleman. Done well by herself."

"Far as we know," added Malvern, more gruff than usual. "She don't write. Don't come a-callin', either. Fact is, we haven't seen nor heard of her for nigh on six—make that seven years."

"She has two fine strapping sons. Full grown now. We went to see her once, but she . . . well. . . ."

"She acted like she was embarrassed to have us around," said Malvern. "Lives in a big house now, with servants and all. Reckon she'd be happier was her father President of these here United States, instead of what he is, an ol' mule skinner."

"Now, Malvern . . ."

"Hell, Eliza. It's true and you know it."

"What about you, Abigail?" asked Eliza, changing the subject. "Where are you from? Do you see your folks?"

"My folks are dead."

"Oh, dear. I'm so sorry." Eliza reached out and put a hand over Chancey's.

Chancey glanced at Torn, a stricken look on her face.

"And my name's not Abigail," she said. "It's Chancey. Chancey Lane."

"Huh?" grunted Malvern. He scratched his stubbled cheek. "I seem to recollect that name."

"I lied to you," confessed Chancey. "I'm sorry. I felt I had to, to get your help. I didn't think you'd help me if you knew who I was . . ."

Malvern slapped his knee. "Of course! Chancey

Lane. The Lady Outlaw!" His narrowed eyes swung to Torn. "Reckon that means you're an owlhoot, too."

"I'm a federal judge."

"Do tell."

"I don't blame you for being skeptical," said Torn. "But what I'm telling you is true. I sincerely hope you'll believe it. And that you'll believe the rest of what I'm going to tell you. Your life may depend on it."

Malvern peered at Chancey. "So all this talk about renegades. Was that straight talk, or crooked?"

"Crooked."

"Then who killed Sheriff Rawlins?"

"I did," said Chancey.

Malvern's gaze flicked to the shotgun over the mantel.

"You don't need it," said Torn. "I'm a judge, and I'm taking Chancey to Broken Bow, to meet up with U.S. Marshals. She's promised to testify against Ash Wheeler and identify all the members of the Blue River Gang."

"Who shot you?" asked Malvern.

"Rawlins did."

"Now why would a sheriff shoot a judge?"

"He was as crooked as a dog's hind leg, Mr. Burkhart."

There was a moment of silence. Malvern looked Torn square in the eye. Torn looked him right square back. Burkhart's fingers drummed the table. It was the only sound in the room. Torn thought he could have cut the tension with a knife.

Finally, Malvern said, "That don't surprise me. I never trusted that sorry son-of-a-gun. I allus suspected he had a hand in the holdup of that big gold shipment about five-year back, over at Calicut Grade."

"He did," said Torn. "He was Wheeler's inside man."

Malvern snorted. "Then I'm glad I didn't take the time to bury him."

"Malvern!" This time Eliza was truly shocked.

"I'm grateful for your help," said Torn, "but being good Samaritans has put you both in danger."

"How come?"

"Because the whole Blue River Gang is out looking for us."

Malvern got up, crossed the room, and took down his shotgun.

"Bring 'em on," he said.

CHAPTER 17

TORN SHOOK HIS HEAD.

"No," was all he said.

"You got a choice?" asked Malvern.

"We'll ride out."

"Oh, you will? You figure you can ride? You'll get maybe a quarter-mile, if that, before you eat dust. A man with a head wound like you got can't ride."

"Yes, I can. It isn't open for debate."

"Let's find out. I'll saddle you up a horse and you ride out a ways and then back."

"Malvern!" exclaimed Eliza.

Torn stood up. "I appreciate what you folks did for me. I reckon Chancey and I will be leaving now . . ."

"You're in no condition to travel," said Eliza.

"I've been hurt worse. If Ash Wheeler and his

83

bunch swing by here on our trail, I reckon they'll let you be once they find out we're gone."

"I wouldn't bet on it," said Chancey.

Torn gave her a long, hard look.

"Ash Wheeler hasn't got a decent bone in his body," said Chancey. "He's a cold-blooded killer, to boot. He wouldn't think twice about killing these two nice people, if for no other reason than that they helped us."

"Then I guess the two of you will have to go with us," Torn told the Burkharts.

"Not on your life," snapped Malvern. "By God, I just got through tellin' you we've made this our home for better'n half our lives. I ain't gonna be run out of my home by a pack of no-account rascals."

"Now look . . ."

"It ain't open for debate."

"Think about your wife."

"My Liza's as good a shot as any man in this state. We've fought off renegades and road agents before, just the two of us."

"The odds are too great. Wheeler has twenty, maybe thirty, hardcases riding with him."

"We're not leavin'," said Malvern, gripping the shotgun so hard his knuckles were white. "Don't try to make us, Judge. That would be poor judgment."

Exasperated, Torn looked at Eliza, but he could tell by her expression that she was as adamant as her husband.

"Well," he said, sitting back down, "that puts me in a bind. I've taken on the job of getting Chancey at least as far as Broken Bow, where, if all goes according to plan, I'll turn her over to U.S. Marshals. But I don't feel right leaving you folks to face Ash Wheeler alone."

"Four guns are better than two," said Malvern.

"What?"

"Way I hear it told, Miss Chancey Lane is a heck of a shot. You look like you know your way around a shooting iron, Judge. There's strength in numbers. Ain't that the way it goes? So we should stick together."

"This isn't your fight."

"Sure nuff is. As a law-abiding citizen, it's my duty to take on outlaws like Wheeler and his bunch. Besides, you wouldn't get far. Not in your condition."

Torn glanced at Chancey.

"I want to stay," she said.

Torn didn't like it. They had as much as signed the Burkharts' death warrants by being here. Of course, he had no say in the matter of his presence here, but that didn't make this particular pill any easier to swallow.

"It's settled, then," said Malvern. "Now, I don't know about you folks, but I'm hungry. Feels like my belt buckle's stuck to my spine."

"The stew's ready," said Eliza.

She and Chancey brought the food to the table. It was simple fare: stew, brown bread, and coffee, but Torn had never tasted better. He hadn't realized how hungry he was until the food was placed in front of him. He had seconds. Eliza commented that this was a good sign.

"A hearty appetite means you'll mend," she said.

After they had finished, Chancey jumped up and helped Eliza gather the crockery.

"Don't worry about those, dear," said Eliza.

So fervent was Chancey in the desire to do her share of kitchen duty that Eliza relented with a gentle smile.

"That's very kind of you, Ab . . . I mean, Chancey."

"You're not angry at me for lying?"

"You had good intentions."

"But I'm supposed to be an outlaw. A fallen woman."

"We should be judged by what we do today, not what we've done in the past."

"Reckon I'll step out and have me a chew," said Malvern. "Want to try a little fresh air on for size, Judge?"

"I'd like that."

"Stay out of the sun," Eliza warned Torn.

Torn smiled. "Yes ma'am."

He and Malvern stepped outside. Torn noticed that Burkhart was hauling that old English double-barrel along.

Once out in the shade of the porch, Malvern leaned the shotgun against the wall, fished out a plug of Wedding Cake tobacco from the pocket of his overalls, and trimmed off a corner with a Barlow knife. He offered knife and plug to Torn.

"Care for a chaw?"

"No thanks."

"Ma won't let me spit in the house. Got a spittoon. But I missed once, twenty-five years ago, and I ain't been allowed to try it again."

Torn took a look around. There was rocky high ground behind the house, the rolling prairie in front. A corral off to one side, shaded by a few scrawny cottonwoods. A rickety barn. A blacksmith's set-up in the striped shade of a pole ramada. A creek ran along the far side of the corral then curled around in front of the house as it worked its way out of the hills and into the prairie.

"Year-round water," said Malvern, noting Torn's careful attention to his surroundings. "Good springs up in them hills. Sweetwater. Rock pools. One reason the stage line was routed through here. Also the reason Liza and me ain't strangers to trouble. Injuns used to water here. Road agents, too."

It was midmorning, but already hot—the air like liquid fire in the lungs. Torn felt dizzy and a little nauseated. He sagged into a convenient rocking chair.

A mangy old white hound came stiff-legged around the corner of the house. It sniffed at Torn, wagged its tail with polite enthusiasm, collapsed on the weathered planks of the porch floor, and laid its grizzled muzzle between Torn's boots.

"That's ol' Ranger," said Malvern fondly. "He's going on fifteen. Gone mostly blind, but his smeller still works. Used to be one helluva huntin' dog." There was a trace of sadness in his voice, for he knew that, inevitably, and some day soon, a tried and true friend would be gone. "You must be okay. Ranger's the best judge of character I ever met."

But Torn was hardly listening. His steelcast gray eyes scanned the horizon.

"How far to Reddon Springs?" he asked.

"About two hours by wagon."

"They've got a telegraph there?"

"Sure they do. What you've got in mind, Judge? You're up to something."

"Muhammad and the mountain," murmured Torn.

"Huh?"

"Since I can't get to the U.S. Marshals in Broken Bow, I guess I'll get them to come here."

"How long you reckon it'll take them?"

"I figure we'll see Wheeler and his gang first."

CHAPTER 18

"I'M LEAVING," TORN TOLD HER.

"You're not coming back for me, are you?"

"Of course I'm coming back," said Torn, disgusted, because it seemed like a dumb thing for her to say. "For God's sakes, Chancey."

Her chin came up and her gold-flecked hazel eyes flashed. "Not that I really care."

Standing there, she looked so lost and alone that Torn's anger, irrational to begin with, quickly subsided. Then he had an urge, also irrational, to put his arms around her. That also subsided, though not quite so quickly.

"I've got to get a wire off to Broken Bow. When those federal marshals get there and read the telegram they'll come here."

"How long?"

Torn shook his head. "All the way here from Lincoln? Five more days, I'd guess."

She didn't answer. Didn't have to. He knew what she was thinking. It was too long.

"Anyway," said Torn, "Malvern says there's a homestead a few miles up the road. The man there's named Miller. He came by here yesterday, while I was unconscious."

"I remember. He'd been out hunting. Had a deer in the back of his wagon. He told the Burkharts he'd bring them some venison."

"He'll take my message on into Reddon Springs and get the telegram off," said Torn. "Malvern says I can trust him. Reckon I'll have to. That way I can be back here a lot quicker than if I went into town myself."

"But you can't ride. Why not let Mr. Burkhart go?"

"It's just as dangerous out there on the road as it is right here. Maybe more. At least here the three of you can fort up. Malvern's hitching up a wagon. He doesn't think I'd last there and back if I rode a horse. He might be right. I'm not taking the chance."

"You're taking a big chance."

"No choice. I'll be back."

She nodded. "I'll be here."

Torn figured she would be. Where would she run, if she were so inclined? She was smart enough to realize it was safer here with the Burkharts then it would be floating her own stick.

Malvern came in. "Your rig's ready, Judge."

Torn took his leave of Chancey and Eliza Burkhart and stepped outside with Malvern, carrying the Winchester 44/40.

"Reason I wanted you to take this rig," said Burkhart, "those mules'll turn around and come home if you happen to pass out."

"Keep your eyes peeled."

"Same to you."

Torn climbed onto the wagon's bench, took up the leathers, and whipped the two-mule hitch into motion. His shotgun shoulder-racked, standing there in the porch shade, Malvern spat a stream of tobacco juice and watched him go.

At that very moment, not too very many miles away, Ash Wheeler sat on his heels near the body of Sheriff Ben Rawlins. The corpse was bloated. Flies were swarming. The stench was pretty bad. A few of the twenty riders who sat their horses behind him were having trouble with their mounts, who didn't much care for the smell. As the riders approached, the vultures had reluctantly taken wing. Now they were perched in the trees above, red-eyed and bloody-beaked. What they had done to Rawlins wasn't pretty. Even hardened hombres like the Blue River Gang felt their stomachs turn.

But none of it seemed to bother Wheeler in the least.

Standing, hands on hips, he looked around at the ground a moment, then yelled, "Choctaw!"

One of the outlaws dismounted and led his cayuse out of the pack of horsemen. He was a short, stocky, bow-legged character. His bronze complexion and long greasy black hair testified to the Indian half of his pedigree. Bandoliers filled with cartridges for his old Spencer carbine criss-crossed his chest.

His name was Choctaw Charley Black, notorious horse thief and consummate tracker. It was the latter talent Wheeler wanted him to employ now.

Ash just turned to Choctaw and said, "Tell me what happened here."

Choctaw nodded. He started walking around the camp, his eyes scanning the rocky ground, occasionally kneeling to get a closer look. Wheeler watched him work. The outlaw named Calder walked up to the bandit leader and glanced at what was left of Rawlins. He winced—he couldn't help himself.

"Was this your two-bit badgetoter, boss?"

"You're not as jack-ass dumb as you look, Calder."

"Should we plant him?"

"Got something against buzzards? Want those poor critters up there to starve?"

Calder glanced up into the trees—and winced again.

A bit later, Choctaw returned to Wheeler.

"One man, one woman, camp here," said the half-breed. "Then this man come. The other man is shot, but I think he lives."

"Too bad," remarked Wheeler.

"Then woman rode off. She comes back with another man in a wagon. I think the man who was shot rides in the wagon when they go from place."

"How long ago?"

"Yesterday. Then another man come, today, on horse. Follows wagon tracks."

"Big Jack," sighed Wheeler. "Well, if Torn's hurt that ought to slow 'em down. Mount up, boys. I think we're near the end of the trail."

Calder and Choctaw remounted. Wheeler paused for one final glance at Rawlins.

"Thanks, Sheriff," he said, sardonicly. "I'll finish that sonuvabitch for you."

CHAPTER

19

TORN KEPT HIS EYES OPEN ALL THE WAY TO THE HOME-
stead of the man named Miller. He half-expected to
meet up with the entire Blue River Gang. They
couldn't be too far behind.

But nothing happened. He didn't see a living soul.

Before long he was glad he'd brought the wagon.
The heat made his head hurt. Every jounce and jiggle
of the wagon gave him a fresh dose of pain. He felt
dizzy, and a few times thought he was going to pass
out. The wagon wasn't the smoothest ride in the
world, but it was smoother than going it on horse-
back.

It was a relief to see the Miller place up ahead.
There wasn't much to it—a weather-beaten clapboard
house, a scattering of outbuildings, a well, a stock pen,
a couple of scraggly trees offering a modicum of wel-

come shade from the blistering summer sun. A chorus of locusts were buzzing in the trees. A single buzzard sailed the wind currents, a black speck against the sun-bleached white sky.

As he drew near, Torn expected to see someone emerge from the house. Life out here was lonely, and having any company to talk to was always an event. But even when the wagon rolled in under the trees, no one appeared to greet Torn.

A sudden premonition of danger made him climb the reins and stop the mules in the hitch before the wagon got close to the house.

Something was wrong.

He scanned the homestead with steel-gray eyes suspiciously narrowed.

Nothing appeared out of the ordinary. The place had a deserted feel. There were a couple of horses in the pen. Maybe the Millers had gone into Reddon Springs. No, there was a buckboard at the side of the house. It was unlikely they would have more than one wagon. Didn't appear that the Millers were all that prosperous.

"Hello, the house!"

No response. Over in the pen, one of the horses whickered. Torn told himself he was being paranoid. If Wheeler and his gang were here he would know it by now—the air would be full of hot lead. So he stirred up the mules and drove the wagon closer to the house.

As the wagon drew near the well, both mules started acting up. Torn noticed the well bucket lay on its side on the ground. Again he stopped the wagon. This time he climbed down, bringing the Winchester with him. He noticed splotches of blood on the stones.

An experimental pull on the crank informed him that something very heavy hung on the end of the well-rope.

Torn cautiously peered over the edge and down into the well.

He couldn't see anything.

Steeling himself, he put the Winchester down and channeled his strength to the task of cranking up the rope.

There was a dead man on the end of the rope, hanging by his wrists. He had been brutally beaten, and then almost blown in half by a shotgun blast at close range.

Torn had seen more than his share of corpses in three years of war, a year and a half in a hellhole prison camp and a dozen years on the frontier pursuing an often violent profession. But seldom had he seen worse than this. He tasted bile, swallowed hard.

A glance skyward showed him that the one buzzard he had seen earlier had company now. Two more. They were gathering. They knew there was death down below.

He wasn't sure what to do with the corpse. This, he surmised, was Miller. Of course, he'd never seen Miller, but even his own mother probably wouldn't recognize the remains. A proper burial would be the decent thing, but for the time being Torn cranked the body back down into the well. That, at least, would foil the buzzards.

Retrieving the Winchester, Torn cautiously approached the house.

The house had been built dogtrot style. Torn ventured into the covered walkway separating the two sections. There were two doors, one into each part of the house. The door to the right was open. Torn opened it wider with the Winchester's barrel, peered into the kitchen area, rough-hewn table in the center, cold black fireplace opposite the door.

There was a second room behind the kitchen. Torn crossed to its door, listened a moment, then pushed it open. It swung free about a foot, no more. Torn pushed harder. The door wouldn't budge. He put his shoulder into it. The body sprawled on the floor, which had kept the door from swinging full open, moved enough to allow Torn entry into the room.

She lay on her belly, legs and arms akimbo. The back of her head had been bashed in. Her eyes were wide open, staring at nothing and seemed filled with surprise. There was a big pool of blood beneath her head. Flies were wallowing in it.

Torn bleakly scanned the room. It was small, barely large enough to accommodate a narrow iron bedstead hosting a cornhusk mattress covered with a ragged quilt and a rickety cupboard filled with dishes and linen. A straw doll sat on the sill of the solitary window and stared at him with button eyes as lifeless as those of the woman on the floor.

His first thought was that renegades, like the four he'd had a run-in with a few days ago, were responsible. Not even Wheeler and his longriders would do this, not without reason. And what reason could they have to murder innocent folks? Robbery? What did the Millers have that the Blue River Gang would want?

But if renegades had done this why hadn't they looted the place? Stolen the horses in the pen? They were certainly capable of killing a man just to have the shirt off his back, but it was obvious this place hadn't been ransacked.

A telltale floorboard creaked.

Torn started to turn.

"Don't," growled Big Jack Eades. "Get shed of that rifle 'fore you turn around."

Torn didn't know who was behind him—and he wasn't going to find out unless he could turn around —and he wouldn't live long enough to find out if he turned around with the Winchester still in his grasp.

All he could do was obey.

So he dropped the Winchester on the cornhusk mattress.

"Step back out of that room, slow like."

Torn did as he was told. Two backward steps brought him across the threshold into the kitchen.

"Now hold your arms out level with your shoulders."

Torn raised his arms.

Big Jack eased closer. Planted the sawed-off barrels of his scattergun in the small of Torn's back. Plucked the Colt out of Torn's holster. Then he backed away.

"Now you can turn around."

Torn did. Recognized Big Jack as one of the outlaws with whom he'd traded lead in Lonesome Pine.

This was the one that had killed Sheriff Logan.

"I see you remember me," said Big Jack. "That's good. Names Eades. Jack Eades. You kilt my son Johnny back there in Lonesome Pine. Sent him to hell. Now I'm gonna send you down there to keep him company."

CHAPTER 20

"DID YOU DO THIS?" ASKED TORN, COLDLY.

"Yeah."

"Then I think *you* should go to hell."

"I didn't want to kill the woman. But she put up a fight."

"Why?" snapped Torn. "These people didn't do anything to you. They didn't deserve to die."

"I came lookin' for you."

"Here?"

"I seen blood. On the road. Figured it was yours. I figured by the sign back at that creek, where that starpacker's layin', that you were hurt."

Torn put it all together in a flash. Jack Eades had been tracking him from the creek, knowing by the sign that he was being transported in a wagon. This had brought Eades straight to the Burkhart's place.

Probably sometime last night. Otherwise, Burkhart probably would have seen him. Yes, last night—as Torn was laid up, unconscious, in bed, this cold-blooded killer on a vengeance trail had passed a stone's throw away.

And had kept on going. Because the man Miller had been in a wagon, too, with a fresh-killed deer bleeding in the wagon bed, and had passed that way earlier on his way up the road and home. Jack Eades had seen the blood at the creek and the blood on the road and had made a wrong conclusion. So he had followed the blood trail—right past the Burkhart's place, and it had brought him here.

"I figured the man was hiding you and Chancey," continued Eades. "So I tried to persuade him to talk. But he kept holding out on me."

"You bastard," said Torn. "He didn't know anything."

"Then what are you doing here? Where's Chancey?"

"You'll never know."

Big Jack shrugged. "I don't really care, to tell you the honest truth. You're the one I'm lookin' for. I reckon I'll make you die slow, Judge. Think I'll blow off both your legs, one at a time. Then I'll just watch you bleed to death."

Torn still had the saber-knife. This was why he had taken long ago to wearing it in a custom made shoulder-rig of his own design, beneath the black frock coat. On more than one occasion adversaries had mistakenly believed him to be unarmed and helpless once he'd been divested of the Colt and Winchester. It had been too late for them when they found out otherwise.

Big Jack was gloating. In a way, he was off his

guard. He thought Torn was at his mercy, and he was enjoying every minute of it. If he expected Torn to do anything at all it was to make a dive for the door into the room where the dead woman lay—and where he had left the Winchester.

Instead, Torn lunged under the table in the center of the room. Rolling, he kicked the table over, and flung an arm over his face as the shotgun blast splintered the worn planks that formed the top of the table. He felt the sting of double-ought pellets or splinters in his thigh and side, he wasn't sure which. But it was of no consequence. Drawing the saber-knife, aware that Big Jack had only triggered one barrel, he grabbed a leg of the table and stood the table up on its end as he stood up, then shoved it into the outlaw. Big Jack staggered backward. The table fell forward into him. He lost his balance and fell, the table coming down on top of him. The shotgun roared again. This time the load gouged out a big chunk of floor. Torn dropped onto the table, on one knee, and drove the saber-knife between two planks and into Big Jack's chest. Eades roared. Torn pushed for all he was worth, snarling like a wild animal himself, driving the blade into Big Jack as far as it could go. He heard ribs crack. Big Jack's boot heels drummed against the floorboards.

Then Big Jack was still.

Torn got up, feeling suddenly drained of strength. His head was pounding. He pushed the table out of the way and dragged his Colt out of the dead man's belt, noticing that Big Jack had lost his glass eye. It was rolling across the uneven floor. Torn holstered the Colt. Wiping the blade of the saber-knife clean on Big Jack's trouser leg—the outlaw's shirt was soaked with blood from the mortal wound in his chest—he secured the weapon in its sheath.

Going out onto the dogtrot between the two halves of the house, Torn sat on the porch steps and rested, head in his hands, until the pain had subsided to the point of being almost bearable.

Later, he found a shovel and dug two graves. He was scarcely in any condition for hard labor, and he felt the urgent need to get back to the Burkhart place as quickly as possible, but he couldn't just leave the Millers the way they were. They deserved a decent burial. So he grit his teeth and endured the pain and got the job done.

He buried the woman first, wrapping her remains in a blanket and carrying her to the gravesite. Then he fetched the dead man out of the well and placed him in the second grave, side by side with the woman.

After filling the graves and packing the dirt down with the flat of the shovel, Torn stood there a moment, wiping sweat off his face. It occurred to him that he ought to say a few words over the dead, but he didn't remember how to pray. Besides that, he had a feeling God had stopped listening to him a long time ago. And sometimes he wondered if there *was* a God west of the Mississippi.

His last task was to drag Big Jack Eades out of the house. He left the outlaw sprawled in the dust in front of the place. Torn wasn't sure why he bothered. He had no intention of spending time or effort planting Eades six feet under. He just didn't want Eades in the Miller house, even dead. Let him feed the buzzards.

His work done, Torn climbed aboard the wagon and whipped up the mules.

He debated whether to continue on to Reddon Springs or return to the Burkhart place.

If Eades had come this far, could Wheeler and the rest of the Blue River Gang be far behind?

Torn couldn't shake the feeling that he had better get back to Chancey and the Burkharts. He was determined to persuade the Burkharts to leave their home and seek refuge in town.

He just hoped it wasn't too late.

CHAPTER 21

Torn met Malvern long before he got to the Burkhart place.

In fact, Malvern met him halfway, on a lathered, hard-run blazed sorrel—the horse Chancey Lane had ridden out of Lonesome Pine.

"My God," breathed Torn. "What happened?"

"They came, not long after you left."

"They? Wheeler and his gang?"

"I reckon Wheeler was among 'em. I didn't get close enough to ask 'em all their names."

"Chancey . . . Eliza . . ."

"Hell, Judge. You think I'd still be above snakes if something had happened to them? What do you think I am?"

Torn's heart was beginning to beat normally again.

"You better tell me what happened."

"I will. But first, you better get this wagon off the road. Some of them owlhoots are about a mile behind me and a-comin' this way."

Torn looked around. There wasn't a tree or a rock to hide behind as far as the eye could see.

"Follow me," said Malvern.

He led Torn off the road. About three hundred yards to the north was a ravine. Malvern dismounted and coaxed the mules down the steep slope. Torn stood by, holding the blazed sorrel. Burkhart managed to get mules and wagon down into the ravine all in one piece, which was no mean feat. Then Torn recalled that Burkhart had once been a mule skinner and freighter.

With wagon, mules, horse, and themselves out of sight of the road, Malvern cut himself a chew from his plug of Wedding Cake and told Torn what had happened.

"Right after you left I got to thinkin' it might be smart to move Chancey and Eliza away from the house. Back up in the hills, near one of them sweetwater springs I told you about, is a cave. Liza and me used it once before, when a bunch of Pawnees came through here on the rampage. You can't hardly find it unless you know right where to look. I made sure they were snugged away in there—left 'em that dun horse of yours—and started back to the house . . ."

"Why didn't you stay with them?"

"I was gonna wait for you. I couldn't very well leave you a note tellin' where we were, now could I?"

"No. I guess that wouldn't have been too smart."

"I topped a rise and seen 'em, millin' around the house. Must be about twenty of 'em. So that's when I circled around to the road and came looking for you. I seen dust behind me. Way I figure it, some or all of 'em are headin' for town. Guess they think that's where you went. Did you talk to Miller?"

"No."

"No? Why not?"

"He was dead."

"Dead?" Malvern couldn't believe his ears.

"I'm sorry."

"Why? Did you do it?"

"Well, I reckon I was responsible. You see, there was a man name of Jack Eades. Rode with Wheeler. I killed his son back in Lonesome Pine. Eades came looking for me on his own stick. He passed your place by and paid a call on the Millers. He made a mistake. Followed the wrong trail."

"He killed Miller? And . . ."

"Yes," snapped Torn, haunted by the vivid memory of the dead woman. "They're both dead."

They were sitting, side by side, on the steep embankment. Malvern took off his hat, ran his fingers through thinning hair, stared pensively at the ground between his feet for a spell.

"Did you kill the sonuvabitch?" he asked, quietly.

"Yes, I did."

Burkhart nodded. "Good. He deserved to die. Eye for an eye. That's a good law. Why waste time on a trial and a hanging for a no-good bastard like that?" He glanced at Torn. " 'Course, you being a judge and all, maybe you don't see it that way."

"It was an open-and-shut case."

"How many outlaws have you done in, Judge?"

"Too many." Torn's voice was bleak. "Too many . . ."

They heard the thunder of galloping horses. Climbing to the top of the bank, they peered over the rim.

Men were riding down the road, trailing a plume of pale dust.

"How many you count?" asked Malvern.

"Fifteen."

"You see Wheeler?"

"Can't tell. I haven't met him—yet. All I have to go by is a picture on a wanted poster."

"There's more than that. Reckon some are still at my place?"

"I reckon," said Torn. "Just in case somebody shows up."

They watched the riders until they were out of sight. The thunder faded away.

"What do we do now?" asked Malvern.

"Go back and get Chancey and your wife."

"Nobody's gonna run me off my place, Judge."

"Now look . . ."

"No. You look. If some of them polecats are hangin' around my house, I aim to clear 'em out. If you don't want to buy in, that's okay with me. But it's my home and hearth and by God I'll fight to keep it. Maybe you think just because I'm a little long in the tooth you'd do better not to side with me, and I reckon I couldn't blame you for feeling that way . . ."

"I don't," said Torn. "In fact, I can't think of anybody I'd rather have backing me up."

"Well, then, that's settled," said Malvern. He stood and started down toward the horse, mules, and wagon, the shotgun shoulder-racked. "Come along, Judge. We've got to teach Ash Wheeler and his kind that they can't ride roughshod over decent folk anymore."

CHAPTER

22

THEY STOPPED ABOUT A MILE SHY OF THE HOUSE AND switched—Torn taking the horse and Malvern climbing up into the wagon.

"I don't think this is a good idea," said Torn.

"You done said that before. But you ain't come up with a better one, have you?"

Torn grimaced. "No."

"I don't reckon they'll kill me right off. They'll want to know if I know where you and Chancey are. Miller wasn't killed right off, was he?"

"No. He was beat half to death first."

Malvern shrugged. He was cool as a cucumber. "Let 'em do their worst. That'll keep 'em busy while you Indian-up on 'em."

Torn shook his head in wonder. "You're one tough customer, Mr. Burkhart."

"Call me Mal. Hell, hoss, if we're gonna die together we might as well be friends."

Torn climbed into the saddle. He checked his timepiece. Then he leaned over and stuck out a hand. Malvern shook it. "Give me half an hour," said Torn.

"See you later, Judge."

Torn just nodded. Malvern tossed him his Winchester rifle, and Torn left the road. He headed north, about a half-mile, then turned west, to face the setting sun, a red ball in the sky, dropping fast to the rimrock of the high ground behind the Burkhart place.

He came to the creek that wandered down out of the hills to circle around the Burkhart homestead. Dusky shadows filled the creek bed. Dismounting, he tied the sorrel to a shrub and proceeded on foot, keeping to the rocky creek bed. The course took him around in front of the house. If he stayed in a crouch he could keep out of sight of anyone in or near the house.

Just ahead was a bridge of heavy wooden timbers, where the road to Reddon Springs crossed the creek. Torn took a breather under the bridge. He wondered idly how far they'd had to haul all this timber. There was more wood in this bridge than Torn had seen all day.

He checked the action of the Winchester and blew dust out of the breech. Then he waited for Malvern. He consulted his stemwinder. Almost half an hour had passed since he'd parted company with Malvern.

Right on time, Burkhart came along. The wagon trundled across the bridge. Torn climbed to the top of the embankment and took a cautious look. Malvern was checking the mules to stop the wagon in front of the house. There was no sign of the longriders. They had hidden their horses. But Torn knew they were here. He could feel it in his bones. He was an old warhorse, and he knew when the enemy was near. But then that instinct had failed him once today . . .

Malvern was climbing down off the wagon when a man stepped out of the front door onto the porch. The rifle he held at hip level was aimed rock-steady at Burkhart.

"Leave that shotgun," advised the outlaw, "and come inside, old man."

Malvern had been reaching for the shotgun in the wagon box. He froze, as if startled, then turned slowly to face the man.

"Who the blue blazes . . . ?"

The longrider jacked a round into the rifle's breech. It was an action that spoke a lot louder than words. He was not going to cut Malvern any slack.

"Awright," grumbled Burkhart, crotchety. "Mighty kind of you to invite me into my own house."

According to plan, Malvern had parked the wagon directly between the bridge and the house. Torn figured he could use the wagon as cover to get closer. Also, working to his advantage was the fact that the day was rapidly drawing to a close. The sun had descended behind the hills beyond the house, and the long purple shadows of twilight had gathered.

Torn wondered how many men were in the house. Malvern had said he'd seen about twenty outlaws, and they'd seen fifteen making tracks for Reddon Springs. That left five. Torn figured one, maybe two, had probably been assigned to tend the horses, which had obviously been removed from the immediate vicinity, but probably within sound of a gunshot signal. At the signal the horsetender—or horsetenders—would bring up the mounts of those at the house.

Question was, were the other three or four long-riders all in the house?

Torn was quite aware that there could be one or two lurking out here, under cover. But there was only one way to find out.

So he went over the rim of the creek bank and moved, in a deep crouch, toward the wagon, confident that no one could see him from the door or windows of the house, even if they were looking.

But as he got closer he could tell Malvern was keeping them pretty well occupied.

"We know they were here." This was the man who had stepped out of the house to greet Malvern. "We tracked 'em this far. Or I should say Choctaw yonder did. He could track an ant over a rock."

So there were at least two outlaws inside, thought Torn, crouched behind the wagon a stone's throw away from the house.

"They were here," conceded Malvern. "I ain't deny-ing that. But they're gone. Came and went yesterday. I don't know where they were headed. I could see them two was trouble, and I wanted no part of it. I mind my own business. That's the only way to stay alive out here. I've learned that much."

"Torn was wounded. Ain't that so, Choctaw? And he was laid up here. Signs of that all over this house."

"I didn't say he wasn't hurt. But he wasn't hurt so bad that he couldn't move on."

"A woman lives here. Where's she?"

"That's my wife, Liza. She's in town. I just got back from taking her. One of her friends is ailin', and Liza's gonna stay with her a spell, till she gets back on her feet."

Torn smiled. Malvern Burkhart could think fast, no doubt about that.

"I think you're lyin'," growled the outlaw, his tone of voice heavy with menace.

"I'm telling you they come and gone. You see 'em around here anywhere? You done tore up my whole house."

"Maybe your telling the truth, maybe not. There's one way to find out. Calder, tie him up. I'm gonna work him over a bit. If he's singing the same song after that, maybe I'll be persuaded."

Calder. So that made three in the house. Torn felt better. It was time to move in. He didn't want them to lay a hand on Malvern Burkhart.

So he came around the wagon, heading for the front door of the house.

He saw the flash of the muzzle out of the corner of his eye. Heard the bullet whistle past his head a fraction of a second later. Then the gunshot split the dusky silence. He dived under the wagon. The man who had been concealed over by the corral fired twice more. The mules in the hitch jerked against their traces. Torn was almost run over as the wagon moved, leaving him without cover. The outlaw was coming toward him, his pistol spitting hot lead. Torn rolled over once, aimed, and fired. He rolled again, working the Winchester's lever action, fired a second time. A bullet kicked dirt in his face, partially blinding him. Again he rolled, working the rifle's action as he did, and fired a third time with his elbows planted and the rifle butt plate snug against his shoulder. The outlaw staggered backward. Then he half-turned and fell flat on his face.

Torn got to his feet, turned toward the house . . . in time to see the outlaw who had come out to meet Malvern emerge a second time.

Now he had a burly arm around Burkhart's throat in a choke hold.

This kept Malvern in front of him, a human shield. He was aiming a revolver at Torn as he took a step forward onto the porch. This allowed a stocky, Indian-looking character—whom Torn immediately assumed was the man named Choctaw—to exit the house and take up a position to one side of him. This outlaw was pointing a Spencer carbine at Torn. The third long-rider, armed with a rifle, stayed just inside the door-way.

It was the third one who spoke first.

"That's him. That's Judge Torn."

Torn's mind flashed back to Lonesome Pine. Could this, then, be the man who had tried to curl his toes with a long shot from the hotel window? That man had been the only member of the bunch Wheeler had dispatched to grab Chancey that Torn had not gotten a look at.

"I figured," said the man holding Malvern. "Judge, I think you better drop that long gun." He turned his pistol on Burkhart, putting the barrel to the old man's head. "If you don't, I'll blow this coot's head clean off."

CHAPTER 23

MALVERN DIDN'T BLINK AN EYE, AND FOR A HANDFUL OF seconds Torn didn't move.

"Your choice," said the man with a choke hold on Burkhart. "Give it up, or the old man dies."

His voice was suddenly very quiet, and Torn took that to be a bad sign. In his experience, the louder and more blustering a man was, the more nervous or scared he was, and the less likely he really wanted to do what he was threatening to do. But this man would put a bullet in Malvern's head, without giving it a second thought, if Torn didn't get rid of the rifle.

But if he did he was finished. He'd been in a similar predicament with Jack Eades and worked his way out of it, by the skin of his teeth, with only a couple of buckshot pellets in his hide, burning now like hellfire. But that had been against one man. He was up against three now. And there was no hope of taking all three of them out if he got shed of the Winchester and the Colt.

Damned if he did, and damned if he didn't. All he could do was pursue the course that would buy him the most time.

He tossed the Winchester away.

"Good," said the outlaw holding the gun to Malvern's head. "Real smart, Judge. Now ease that hogleg out of the holster and throw *it* away."

Torn complied.

"I'll kill him, Haley," snarled the one named Calder, as he brought his rifle up.

"The hell you will," snapped Haley. He didn't take the gun away from Burkhart's head. *This man,* mused Torn, *was no fool.* Menacing Malvern had so far gotten him what he wanted—Torn unarmed—and he wasn't about to discard his ace in the hole. If Torn tried anything, anything at all, Burkhart would die.

"You had your chance at him back in Lonesome Pine, from what Valdez tells me," continued Haley. "He stays alive until we find out where Chancey is."

Torn started to inform Haley it would be a cold day in Hades before he gave that secret up, but Calder beat him to it.

"This one won't talk," sneered the outlaw. "Look at him. He's standing there still looking all high and mighty, unarmed and with three guns pointed at him."

"I'm gonna ask you this just once, Judge," said Haley, and he was talking in that ominously quiet way again. "You tell me where Chancey Lane is, or I'll kill this old man."

Torn had been expecting that. Threatening Malvern's life had worked once for Haley. It was only natural for him to try it again.

"She got away from me," he said.

"What?"

Haley was skeptical. Torn saw as much—it was written all over the longrider's face—and hastened to head that skepticism off before it got somebody— namely Malvern Burkhart—killed.

"She ran off. After that business with Sheriff Rawlins she suddenly developed a case of cold feet. Said there was no way she'd get to Lincoln alive to tell the law all she knew about Wheeler and his gang. She figured her only chance was to break away and hope to run far enough that even Wheeler couldn't track her down."

"You're lying."

Torn shrugged. "I'm telling you the truth. I can't *make* you believe it."

"If that's so, why'd you come back here?"

"She took both horses. This was the nearest place I knew of. Even so, it was an all-day walk."

Haley looked around for Torn's horse. He couldn't see it. Still, he didn't appear altogether inclined to accept Torn's explanation.

Yet Torn had planted a seed of doubt in the outlaw's mind—he could read that much in the man's eyes. As for Malvern, he was watching Torn with a deathly calm look in his eyes. He was waiting for his cue. He figured Torn had some kind of plan in mind to turn the tables on these owlhoots. He was counting on it.

Torn, though, didn't have a plan. He was simply buying time.

Then Ranger came padding around the corner of

the house. The old, mostly-blind hound sniffed the air and wagged its tail in desultory fashion.

"I know you told me you never wanted to see my face again, Burkhart," said Torn.

Malvern blinked. It was an odd comment for Torn to make, under the circumstances. Burkhart was smart enough to realize Torn wanted him to say something, was trying to engage him in conversation.

"Well, I knew you'd drag some trouble along with you," he replied, mustering up some genuine-sounding indignation. "I told you it warn't right, puttin' inno cent folk in the line of fire."

As Torn had hoped, Ranger responded to the sound of his master's voice. Tail still wagging, he clambered up on the porch and crossed to Malvern and Haley. He could smell Malvern, but he was also starting to pick up the scent of strangers. His tail ceased to move back and forth and began to lower, because he could also smell fear, and the fear was coming from Malvern. The lips drew back from Ranger's yellowed fangs. The growl started way down deep, growing in volume, and then exploding in a vicious, snarling bark.

Torn wasn't much of an animal lover, with horses being the one exception. But right then he felt like kissing the flea-bitten mutt.

Apparently, Haley wasn't much of a believer in man's best friend, either, because he kicked out with one foot, and the toe of his boot caught Ranger in the ribs and the dog was bowled over sideways, yelping.

"Hey!" shouted Malvern. "Don't kick my dog, dammit."

"Shut the hell up," yelled Haley.

Ranger was back on all fours again, the hair on his

haunches bristling, and then he attacked, his teeth sinking deeply into Haley's calf.

Haley howled.

Malvern reached up and grabbed the barrel of Haley's pistol, still pressed against his temple, and moved it just enough so that when the outlaw pulled the trigger the bullet plowed into one of the porch uprights instead of Burkhart's skull. Haley's choke hold had loosened as he stumbled sideways, into Choctaw. Malvern reeled away from the muzzle flash going off right in front of his eyes.

Torn lunged for his guns. They were close together on the ground, about ten feet to his right. Since Haley was preoccupied with Ranger, and Choctaw knocked off balance, it was Calder Torn knew he had to worry about first. Calder's problem was that he was still inside the house, behind Malvern and Haley and the half-breed, and it took him precious seconds to line up a shot. Torn hit the ground, rolled on his shoulder, and came up with the Colt.

"Malvern, get down!"

But Burkhart wasn't listening to Torn. He hurled himself through the doorway to grapple with Calder. Torn turned his attention to Choctaw. The breed had recovered his balance, and was swinging that Spencer carbine back up. Torn fanned the Colt's hammer. He was aware that fanning reduced accuracy, but at this range he couldn't miss.

He fired three times. Three times Choctaw was hit. The bullets slammed the breed against the wall of the house. Then he pitched forward, dead.

Ranger was still savaging Haley's leg. The outlaw put his gun to the old hound's head and pulled the trigger.

Aiming more deliberately now, Torn did the same for Haley, killing the longrider outright.

One more, thought Torn, as he started for the door to the house. Calder and Malvern were inside. Torn heard a single shot. He couldn't see what was happening. His heart sank. Had Calder won the fight? He was younger, stronger, meaner than Burkhart . . .

But as he reached the porch, Malvern, unscathed, stepped into view and leaned heavily against the door frame.

"There's blood all over the floor," said Burkhart morosely. "Eliza's gonna kill me."

CHAPTER 24

THEY BURIED OL' RANGER. MALVERN WAS HEART-broken, Torn could tell. But he didn't shed a tear. As they stood over the grave, Torn said, "I'd say that hound of yours saved our lives."

Malvern nodded. "He was a good and true friend. I'll miss him and never forget him."

Torn figured that was just about the best eulogy he had ever heard. Short and sweet and coming from the bottom of the heart.

Walking back to the house, Malvern indicated the dead outlaws with a curt gesture.

"What do we do with them?"

"I don't feel like digging four more graves."

"Neither do I. Reckon it would be the Christian thing to do. That's what Eliza will say. But danged if I ain't feeling mighty un-Christian right now. Bothers me some, but I cain't help it. Wonder where that fifth man went to?"

"I don't think he'll try us on his own. My guess is he's going after Wheeler and the rest."

They loaded the dead men into the wagon, and were just finishing up with that task when the sound of a horse at a gallop reached their ears. Malvern ran to the porch to fetch his shotgun. Torn grabbed up his Winchester and searched the darkness for sight of the rider, wondering if he'd been wrong about that fifth hellion.

But it was Eliza and Chancey, riding double on the dun horse Malvern had left in their keeping.

Riding behind Eliza, Chancey executed a running dismount and launched herself at Torn, throwing her arms around his neck.

"You're alive!" she exclaimed. "You came back!"

Flustered, Torn gently but firmly extricated himself from the lady outlaw's enthusiastic embrace.

"I told you I would," he replied, brusque.

Chancey was hurt by his standoffish attitude, but she hid it well. Beyond her, Eliza had dismounted and joined Malvern, giving Burkhart a hug.

"I told you to stay up yonder in them hills till I came to fetch you," scolded Malvern. He was pleased to see his wife, but irritated by her failure to follow his instructions.

"We heard shooting," she said, glanced impassively at the bodies piled in the wagon. "Chancey was bound and determined to come see what had happened. I tried to talk her out of it, but that child, I swear, Malvern, is almost as stubborn as you are."

"Well, hell yes, there was shootin'. These polecats had done took over the place, and they wouldn't leave.

I asked 'em to, all polite-like, Liza, but they wouldn't listen to reason. So the judge and I had to throw 'em out."

"Are you going to bury them, Mal?"

Malvern sighed. "They're no-good owlhoots."

"Doesn't matter what they did when they were alive, Malvern Burkhart. They're dead now. They deserve a decent buryin'."

"Okay, dammit, I'll haul 'em off a ways and plant 'em. But not tonight."

Chancey had moved to the wagon now, identifying the dead men. Torn had never seen her look so serious.

"Friends of yours?" he asked.

"No. I was just thinking, you've done the Blue River Gang a lot of damage."

"I intend to do more."

"Still think you can get me to Broken Bow?"

"If I don't it won't be for want of trying."

They all went inside. Malvern apologized abjectly to Eliza for the blood. She just shook her head and grimly went to work to clean it up. While Malvern closed the shutters on the windows and barred the door, Chancey brewed up some coffee. Then she helped Eliza. She wasn't squeamish. But Torn thought she seemed more distant, and he knew it was because he had pushed her away a moment ago.

Torn took the saber-knife to the buckshot pellets in his hide. He could get to the one in his thigh by just enlarging the tear in his pants. Teeth clenched, he probed for the double-ought with the point of the saber-knife, cutting into the flesh.

"God A'mighty, Judge!" exclaimed Malvern, turning from his labors to secure the house to see Torn performing surgery on himself. "Hold on just a minute and let me do that for you."

"I can manage."

"Don't argue with me." Malvern took the saber-knife and gave it a curious once-over. "Hell of a weapon. But it ain't worth nothin' for the job at hand. I got a clasp knife with a blade as sharp as my wife's tongue." He flashed a grin at Eliza as he brandished said knife. "But first I'll fetch the medicine."

He dashed into the other room, returned with a bottle of Old Overholt.

"Keep it for medicinal purposes only, of course," he said, with a sly wink. "Ninety-proof tongue oil, Judge. Take a few swigs and then I'll proceed to extract the foreign matter from your hide. That's the way that ol' drunken sawbones over in Reddon Springs talks. Mighty educated man, but he doesn't have a lick of sense, and he drinks up most of the medicine."

Torn downed a couple of slugs of whiskey. It wasn't bourbon, his preference, but it smoothed out the nerves.

"Don't look," advised Malvern. "It'll hurt twice as bad if you do."

But Torn watched him as he deftly extracted the pellet from his thigh.

"Any more?"

"One more." Torn shed his jacket, raised his bloody shirt. Malvern made short work of the second pellet.

"Wounds're a little pizened," said Malvern. "Give me that bottle." He poured the whiskey over both wounds. Torn winced as the whiskey seared his bleeding flesh.

Malvern threw a surreptitious glance across the room at Eliza and Chancey, both of whom were diligently scrubbing the bloodstains out of the puncheon floor.

"I've been wonderin'," murmured Burkhart, "about Ash Wheeler." He kept his voice pitched low, so that the women would not hear.

"What about him?"

"Where do you think he'll go once he finds out you and Chancey aren't in Reddon Springs?"

"I don't think he'll get that far."

"Why not?"

"He's bound to have seen what happened at Miller's place. I reckon he's heading back this way right now."

Alarm flashed in Malvern's eyes. "You reckon?"

Torn nodded grimly.

"What are we gonna do?"

"Only thing we can do. Stand and fight, on our own. Only question is, do we stand here, or up in the hills where you left Eliza and Chancey?"

"You leavin' it up to me?"

Again Torn nodded.

Malvern rubbed his chin, pondering for a moment.

"Well, since you ask, I say we stay put here and make our stand."

"That's what I thought you'd say."

CHAPTER 25

They had plenty of guns, having confiscated all the shooting irons—as well as the ammunition—formerly in the possession of the four dead Blue River Gang members. That gave them six short-guns in all, four rifles, and Malvern's shotgun.

"Judge, I got something you ought to see," said Burkhart.

He enlisted Torn's aid in moving the big table in the main room to one side, then he rolled back the threadbare rug that covered a good portion of the floor where the table had stood. This revealed a trap door, with an iron ring set into a recess. Malvern pulled the door up and open, fetched a lantern, and preceded Torn down a sturdy ladder.

Torn found himself standing in a cellar. A dark, earthy, subterranean smell filled his nostrils. He had to stoop slightly to keep from banging his head against stout beams supporting the floor above. The cellar was smaller than the room overhead. It contained a broken chair, a trunk, a few small casks, an old saddle with leather so worn you could see the wooden "tree" in places.

"Folks said I was crazy to put a cellar in. Helluva job, diggin' down this much in hard ground. But where I came from, we had root cellars. I wanted a place to go when a tornado came, or Injuns. Then, when our daughter came along, Eliza talked me into diggin' a tunnel. Over here."

He went to a corner, grabbed the rope handle on one end of the trunk and pulled it away from the wall, which was made of creosote timber. The trunk had concealed a square hole. Malvern got down stiffly on his hands and knees. Torn did likewise. Burkhart held the lantern at arm's length into the tunnel.

"Where does it go?"

"Out past the corral."

"You dug this yourself?" Torn figured roughly it had to be sixty to seventy feet long.

Malvern nodded. "Took months. Y'see, we had it planned out. If Injuns came, I'd hold 'em off upstairs while Liza and our little girl crawled through here. They'd stand a chance of getting away, if I could keep our visitors busy."

"Ever have occasion to use it?"

"Once. They got off into the hills safe and sound, and I got through with my hair still on 'cause, back then, the stage was still running, and the coach out of Reddon Springs happened along in time to save my bacon."

Torn peered down the tunnel. It was barely big enough for a full-grown man to crawl through.

"It's shored up real good," said Malvern. "Never had it cave in, not in all these many years. The tunnel and this here cellar have lasted long as they have on account of it don't rain much at all in these parts."

"This is good," said Torn.

"Yeah. I reckon the women can slip out if it gets to lookin' like the fight's going against us."

"Or I can go out there and we can catch them in a crossfire."

"You'll get yourself killed, Judge."

Torn stood up and brushed his hands together. "That's bound to happen," he replied. "Someday."

They went back up into the house, leaving the lantern burning down in the cellar, and the trapdoor open.

"I'll take first watch," said Torn. "All of you need to try and get some sleep."

Eliza had stoked up a good fire in the stove. She left the iron poker's tip in the flames. "Keep this going," she advised. "We've got plenty of kindlin'. We can use this iron if anybody gets winged. Just slap it on the wound."

Torn smiled. He was mightily impressed by this stalwart couple. With hardy pioneers like the Burkharts populating the frontier, riffraff like Wheeler and his longriders were doomed.

"Reckon they'll hit us at night?" Malvern asked him.

Torn just shrugged. He had no way of knowing.

Eliza gave Chancey a hug. "Get some rest, dear."

"I'm sorry," said Chancey.

"For what?"

"For this. Being the cause of all this trouble. All this killing—it's my fault."

Eliza squeezed her hand. "Don't give it another thought. We're glad you came. Aren't we, Mal?"

"By God, yes!" exclaimed Burkhart. "It don't matter what you've done in the past, gal. Right now you're trying to do the right thing. We're just happy to help." He turned back to Torn. "You call us if you hear anything, Judge. This is one fight I don't want to miss."

They went to their room. Chancey lingered, just standing there, looking down at the floor, deeply troubled.

"You should get some rest," suggested Torn, "like Eliza said."

"I'm not tired." She went to the stove. "Would you like some coffee?"

"Sure."

She poured him a cup, brought it to him.

"What do you think will happen to me?" she asked. "I mean, assuming you leave any of the gang alive, and I testify against them."

"Not too long ago you didn't think we had a prayer of getting through."

"But if we do."

Torn thought it over. It was the first time he had given the future—anything beyond the next few hours —any consideration.

"I doubt if you'll walk away scot-free, Chancey. I won't lie to you. I expect you'll spend some time behind bars. But I'll do what I can."

"Don't suppose I'd get you for a judge."

He smiled. "You've got a state warrant out on you, aside from federal charges. It's the state judge you'll have to answer to. But they'll take the fact that you've cooperated into consideration. I'll make certain of that."

She went back to the stove, got herself a cup of coffee, and sat down at the table. There were a couple of pistols and rifles on the table. She stared bleakly at them.

"I just don't know how all this happened."

"What?"

"How it got this far? How I got from joining up with that peddler to here. A wanted woman."

"You're still young, Chancey. And pretty. Get back on the straight and narrow and you'll find what you're looking for. You just went down the wrong road. You'll catch some fella's eye. Some hard-working, upstanding young man will come along and . . ."

"But not you."

That gave Torn pause.

"No," he said, at length. "Not me."

"Are you married?"

"In a way."

He took the daguerreotype of Melony out of his pocket and walked over and put it on the table in front of her.

"Who is she?"

"My fiancée."

"She's very lucky."

Torn didn't say anything.

"Where is she?"

"I don't know. I've been looking for her for a long time. Since the war. When I got back home she was gone. People said Yankee deserters had kidnapped her. I trailed them to the Indian Nations. Lost the trail there." He drew a deep breath. It was a little ragged. "I'm not sure I'll ever find her. I used to be. For years

I knew she was just around the bend. In the next town. Or the next. That I'd turn the corner and there she'd be. But now . . . now I'm not sure anymore. Not that I'll ever stop looking. I'll never stop."

"You must love her very much."

"I should never have left her. She promised she'd wait for me when I rode off to fight. And I swore I'd come back to her. I'm going to keep my word."

Chancey stood up. She touched Torn's whisker-stubbled cheek.

"She is very lucky," she said, and then she left him, turning to go to the spare room.

CHAPTER 26

SOMETIME IN THE EARLY MORNING HOURS MALVERN RE-
lieved Torn.

"I'm not tired," said Torn, when Burkhart advised
him to get a little sleep.

"Sure. You look like you've been to hell and back
again. You need to be bright-eyed and bushy-tailed
when those owlhoots ride in. Where's Chancey?"

"Asleep in the spare room." Torn knew she was
sleeping—he had gone to check on her a couple of
times.

"That gal's got a shine in her eye when she looks at
you, Judge."

"Won't happen," said Torn, curtly.

Malvern lifted a bushy eyebrow. He poured himself
some coffee then walked over to one of the windows
and peered out through a gunslot. Torn sat in a chair

131

near the other front window. The room was dark. A single lamp, turned down low, was all the light they dared.

"Kind of stuffy in here, with that stove stoked all night long." remarked Malvern. "Mind if I open this door a bit?"

"I don't think that's a good idea."

"You reckon they're out there? If so, why haven't they hit us? I mean, they're not Injuns, are they? Superstitious about attacking at night cause if one of 'em gets kilt his soul might lose his way to the happy huntin' ground in the darkness."

"Maybe Wheeler wants to wait till dawn, so he can see what he's up against."

Malvern snorted. "You and an old man and two women. I wouldn't think that would give a hardcase like Ash Wheeler pause."

"No point in trying to second guess the enemy," said Torn, standing to stretch stiff joints. "They'll come at us when they're ready."

"Maybe they won't come at all. We've already made the Blue River Gang pay a heavy price. Maybe Wheeler's decided she isn't worth the cost."

"From what I know of Wheeler, he doesn't give a damn about the cost. He thinks Chancey's his property. He owns her, and she's run away and he's going to get her back, if it costs a hundred lives."

"Speakin' of Chancey, what'll happen to her, assuming we all survive?"

Torn grimaced. "She's done wrong. She's taken part in bank robberies and stage holdups. She won't get off scot-free."

Malvern was quiet, deep in thought. There was an Indian blanket draped over a rocking chair in one cor-

ner, Torn spread the blanket on the floor in front of
the cold fireplace and stretched out on it. Closed his
eyes. Tried to turn off his brain, so that sleep would
come. It wasn't the fight looming in the immediate
future that bothered him. No, it was Chancey, and
what would happen to her.

"Eliza and me, we've been doin' some talking," said
Malvern suddenly.

Torn opened one eye. He could only dimly make
Malvern out, across the room, in the chair he had
recently vacated, shotgun across his lap.

"About what?"

"Chancey."

"What about her?"

"I think you ought to leave her here with us."

Torn said nothing.

" 'Course, that's assumin' she'd want to stay."

"You want to take in Nebraska's notorious lady outlaw?"

"She doesn't have to be Chancey Lane. She could
go back to bein' Abigail. What's in a name? And who
says you have to keep a name if it's doing nothing but
making trouble for you?"

"I'm a federal judge. I'm supposed to uphold the
law. And Chancey's broken that law."

Malvern's grunt vocalized strong skepticism.
"Judge, I think you're blowing smoke. You uphold the
law the way you see fit, and don't try tellin' me otherwise, 'cause I won't believe it."

Torn rolled over on his side, putting his back to
Burkhart. He didn't think Malvern could see him
smile in the half-lit gloom, but there was no point in
taking the chance.

"I tell you what," he said wryly. "If we're live this time tomorrow, we'll talk it over some more."

"Fair enough. And we will be. Alive, I mean. I think Wheeler's had enough. I think he's folded. On his way back to the Blue River Breaks."

"Right."

"We wouldn't mind at all havin' her around. Be almost like havin' our daughter back with us. She'd have a shot at makin' a brand new start. Don't you think everybody deserves a second chance, Judge?"

I'd like to have a second chance, thought Torn. *A second chance at making a life with Melony.*

But he was just feeling sorry for himself, and put a halt to it.

He didn't respond to Malvern. Lying still, on his side, his back to Burkhart, pretending he was asleep. He saw no profit in making long-range plans. Not with Ash Wheeler out there somewhere.

Malvern bought his possum-playing and said no more, and Torn suddenly realized he was very tired and soon drifted off to sleep.

Next he knew, Malvern was shaking him awake.

"They're here," whispered Burkhart.

Torn was on his feet in a flash. Rifle in hand, he crossed to the nearest window and looked out through the gunslots in the shutter.

They were on their horses, in a line across the yard, beyond the wagon. In the gray twilight before sunrise, a white cottony mist was clinging to the ground, and Torn could not see them clearly. He counted an even dozen. What about the rest. He and Malvern had counted fifteen on the road to Reddon Springs. And which one was Wheeler? Torn was familiar with the likeness of the outlaw leader on those wanted posters and thought he would recognize Wheeler if he saw him. But he couldn't make out features in the fog and half-light. Five of the riders were holding torches aloft. These were strips of cloth, wrapped around one end of sticks as thick as a man's arm, doused with whiskey, probably, and set ablaze.

"You in the house!"

Torn couldn't tell which one was doing the yelling. But he figured it to be Wheeler.

"Chancey! I know you're in there, darlin'. Here's Ash, honey, come to fetch you home!"

Torn threw a quick glance across the room, to see Chancey standing in the doorway to the spare bedroom, her eyes still sleepy, her face very pale, her body stiff with fear.

"Come on out, Chancey! Judge Torn! Give her up, and I'll let you ride away."

"Which one is he?" whispered Malvern.

"I wish I knew," said Torn.

"Yeah. One shot. Cut the head off the rattler . . ."

"You got one minute!" yelled Wheeler. "Then I'm gonna burn you out."

CHAPTER 27

"HE'S BLUFFING," SAID CHANCEY, WITH QUIET CONVICtion.

"I don't think so," replied Torn. "Mal, you'd better go get Eliza."

"I'm here," said Eliza, emerging from the other room, rifle in hand.

From the other window, Malvern yelled, "Here they come!"

Torn looked out through the gunslots. The Blue River Gang was on the move. Some of the riders were putting spurs to their horses, circling the house. A few of the torch-carriers made straight for the front of the house, past the wagon where Haley and three other dead outlaws lay. Gun-flame flickered in the ghostly haze. Bullets slapped the front of the house, smashed window glass. Torn slid the Winchester's barrel through the gunslots and fired. A rider with a torch, one of those going around the house, somersaulted off the back of his horse. Malvern's shotgun roared. Another outlaw fell. But a couple of those with the burning brands got close enough to hurl the torches onto the porch.

With a strangled growl, Malvern headed for the front door.

He had the bar lifted before Torn could reach him and restrain him.

"They're burnin' my house!" raged Burkhart.

"Don't be a fool!"

Malvern put up a struggle. Torn pushed him roughly away from the door.

"You can build another damned house," rasped Torn. "You've only one life."

"He's right, Malvern," said Eliza.

"Get down into the cellar," said Torn. It was an order, not a suggestion.

Malvern came to his senses. "C'mon, Eliza." He headed for the trap door, pausing to scoop a pistol off the table and stick it in his belt.

Chancey had moved to Malvern's window, taking his place, firing coolly through the gunslots, pistols in both hands, discharging first one and then the other.

Torn could already smell the fire. The house would go up like a tinderbox. Smoke was trickling through the wall boards. The crackle of hungry flames was loud in his ears.

"No time to lose," he told Chancey, the words calm and measured.

"Go on," she said.

"Ladies first."

She gave him a sharp look. "I'm tired of running."

"We're not running," he said, exasperated. "We're pulling back to new lines."

She stared, then burst out laughing. Torn wasn't sure what she found so funny. But she gave him no further argument and went through the trap door. Torn followed. The Burkharts were waiting for them in the cellar.

"Through the tunnel," said Torn curtly. "Mal, you go first."

Burkhart obeyed. Eliza and Chancey went next. Torn paused to listen to the rattle of gunfire overhead. How long before they realized that no one was shooting back?

He squeezed into the tunnel. It was barely wide enough for his broad shoulders. He crawled on hands and knees, dragging the Winchester along, bumped his head once on a shoring timber and almost blacked out. His head wound throbbed mercilessly. He tried to ignore the pain.

There was a small square hatch at the end of the tunnel, covered by about four inches of hardpack. Malvern had lifted it out of the way and helped the women up. Torn was relieved to be out of the tunnel. The others were staring at the house. It was a raging inferno, consumed by fire. The riders milling about were dark shapes sharply silhouetted against the blaze.

"Bastards," muttered Malvern. "Sorry about the cussin', Liza, but this really burns my bacon. Them no-account snakes settin' fire to our home."

"Chancey, you and Eliza stay put, and stay low," said Torn. "Come on, Mal."

Chancey clutched at his arm.

"You come back, Judge, you hear?"

He smiled. "Haven't I always? But if things go bad for us, head back into the hills."

With that he started for the distant house, and the outlaw riders, Malvern beside him.

"Stop shooting!" yelled Ash Wheeler, as he spurred his horse ruthlessly this way and that. *"Dammit, stop shooting!"*

He made a complete circle around the burning house, and eventually got everyone's attention. Once the shooting had slacked off he dismounted, whipped the hat off his head, and hurled it to the ground in a fit of rage. Then he kicked the hat. It sailed toward the house, was picked up by the fire-wind, and swirled into the consuming flames. Wheeler hunkered down on his heels and stared morosely at the blaze.

Valdez ventured closer. The Mexican remained in his saddle. He was afraid Wheeler had gone completely loco.

"What now, boss?" asked Valdez.

Wheeler didn't seem to hear.

"It is over, I think," said Valdez. He was ready to go back to the breaks. There had been a lot of killing— too much, in his opinion, over one lousy woman. "Now we go?"

"They should've come out," muttered Wheeler. "I gave them the chance. Why didn't they come out?"

Valdez shrugged. "Maybe because they knew they were going to die anyway. There is no good way to die. A fire, a bullet, what difference?" He shrugged again.

"I wouldn't have hurt Chancey." Wheeler glanced up at the Mexican. "Well, I wouldn't have," he snapped, as though he had heard Valdez's unspoken thoughts.

"*Si*. Whatever you say, boss. Now we . . ."

The bullet hit him square in the chest and knocked him off his horse. Wheeler jumped up. A sudden flurry of gunfire startled him. Confused, he instinctively reached for the Mexican's horse. His own mount had wandered off. Grabbing the reins, he vaulted into the saddle, looked around. Then he saw them. Coming out of the haze and smoke, over near the corral. One of his men galloped past, blazing away, then slipped sideways off his horse.

Two more riders converged on Torn and Burkhart from opposite directions. Back to back, Torn and the old mule skinner fired almost simultaneously, the boom of a shotgun undergirding the sharp report of the Winchester.

With calm deliberation, Malvern broke open the shotgun, plucked the spent shell casings from the barrels, dug into his overalls for a couple more. A bullet tore into his leg. He stumbled, but kept on, because Torn was moving, and he wanted to stick with the judge. Torn's Winchester was spitting flame and hot lead as fast as he could work the lever action. Burkhart reloaded, looked up, saw a rider crossing in front of him, shooting at him. He swung the shotgun up and cut loose with both barrels. The horse galloped off, its bloody saddle empty.

The few outlaws remaining began to melt away into the morning haze. Torn cast aside the empty Winchester, drew the Colt Peacemaker, sent a few bullets flying after them. Still beside him, Malvern discarded the shotgun and drew his own pistol. Torn looked around for new targets. There were none.

A few seconds of gun fury, he thought, *and eight dead men.*

"It's over," he said hoarsely. "You hit?"

"Just a scratch."

Torn gave Malvern's leg wound a cursory look. "I think it's my turn to dig some lead out of you."

"No offense, Judge, but Liza will do it. The way you use that pigsticker of yours makes me nervous. Liza's done it before. She's an old hand."

"As much trouble as you get into, Mal, I'm not surprised."

Torn moved off to check the dead.

The shooting having stopped, Chancey and Eliza ventured out of the creek. They stuck close to Malvern while Torn methodically prowled the killing ground. When he walked back to them he noticed that Chancey was watching him expectantly, and he figured he knew exactly what she wanted to know.

"Ash Wheeler must have gotten away," he said.

"What about those yonder?" asked Burkhart. "Any of 'em still above snakes?"

"All crossed over but one, and he's not long for this world."

He said it bluntly, without emotion, and it struck Malvern how hard-as-nails this black-clad federal judge really was.

"I'm right glad you're on the side of law and order," said the oldtimer. "There'd sure be hell to pay if you rode the outlaw trail." He turned to his wife. "Well, Liza, looks like we lost every damn thing."

"Malvern Burkhart, stop cussing."

"Lord, woman. We get burned out of our home and you won't even let me swear a little."

"We may be burned out, but we're still alive."

"Yeah. Just have to start all over."

"We can do it. We've done it before, and more than

once. We can do anything we set our minds and hearts to."

"There's a reward for some of these men, I reckon," said Torn. "Seems to me you folks ought to have it, since those owlhoots are responsible."

"Blood money," said Malvern.

"Reward money. Dead or alive. I'll take them into Reddon Springs and collect for you."

"What about you and your share? You did a share of the killing."

"I'm a federal judge. I don't collect rewards. This is my job."

Malvern glanced at Chancey. "What about her, Judge?"

"What about her?"

"Last night, you said if we were still alive today you'd think about what I asked you. Well, we're still alive. Some of us barely."

"What are the two of you talking about?" asked Chancey.

"We want you to stay with us," said Eliza. "If you'd like to, that is."

Chancey was thunderstruck. Speechless, she looked from the Burkharts to Torn and back again.

"Really?" she gasped. "But I'm . . . I'm . . ."

"Don't say it," said Eliza. "Don't say you're no good. It isn't so."

"But I don't deserve . . ."

"We all deserve a second chance," said Malvern. "Not too many of us get one in life. We'd be proud to have you stay, gal, if you're of a mind to."

"Well, yes, of course," said Chancey. Then she looked again at Torn, reading his expression, and her smile faded. "But you're not going to let me stay, are you?"

Torn grimaced. He was wedged painfully between a rock and a hard place. He liked the Burkharts—and, yes, Chancey Lane, too—and he wanted to do this one thing for them all. But there were one or two rules by which he lived, and he just could not bring himself to break them.

"I've got to take you in, Chancey."

All three just stood there, too disappointed for words.

"I can't promise you anything," added Torn, "but I'll do everything I can to get the charges against you dropped. I'll make sure they know you helped me destroy the Blue River Gang."

Chancey nodded. She studied the ground around her feet, unable to look Torn, or the Burkharts, in the eye.

"You never can shake loose of the past, I guess," she said in a small voice.

"No," said Torn, angry at himself and at the situation. "I reckon you can't. Mal, I expect you and Liza will have to stay in Reddon Springs for a spell, until you heal up, and I can get you that reward money."

Malvern just nodded.

"Whatever you say, Judge. You're the law."

Torn could tell that none of them were too happy with him at the moment.

He just shrugged and walked away.

CHAPTER

28

TORN RIFLED THE POCKETS OF THE DEAD MEN. WHAT LIT-
tle hard money he found he put in one of his pockets,
intending to add it to the reward money destined for
the Burkharts as a grubstake to finance their rebuild-
ing. Rifles, guns, and gunbelts he threw in a burlap
sack taken from the tack box over by the corral. He
managed to catch up a couple of the owlhoot horses.
These he tied to the back of the wagon. Horses and
tack could be sold in Reddon Springs, and what didn't
go to the local undertaker to defray the cost of bury-
ing eight dead longriders could also go to the
Burkharts.

While Torn labored to lay the dead men in the bed
of the wagon, Eliza set to work cutting the bullet out
of her husband's leg, using Malvern's clasp knife.
Chancey, on her knees beside the oldtimer, held his

hand tightly. Mal grimaced and groaned as Eliza probed the wound with the slender blade, but he did not cry out.

"Wish they hadn't burnt up all my whiskey," lamented Malvern. "I could sure use a shot of ninety-proof painkiller right about now."

"I could put it to better use cauterizing this wound," replied Eliza.

Instead, after removing the bullet, she fetched a revolver from the burlap sack, loaded it, fired it six times, and then slapped the hot barrel on the wound.

Torn found the sorrel down by the creek, where he had left it the day before. He filled the canteen from the Burkhart's well and told the others he was riding out to do a little scouting.

"You all stay here and rest up," he said. "I reckon I'll be back in a few hours."

"Are you going after Ash?" asked Chancey.

"No. I just want to know what the Blue River Gang —what's left of it—is up to."

It didn't take him long to cut their trail. Four riders in all. Their sign pointed west. Back toward the breaks of the Blue River? Had Ash Wheeler given up? Was he finally admitting defeat?

Midmorning found Torn at a place where the tracks clearly showed the outlaws had stopped for a short while. They had dismounted to let their horses breathe. Torn found black spots of blood on the rocky ground. So one of them was wounded, and badly, by the looks of it. There looked to have been a scuffle. One rider had gone off to the north. The others had continued westward. Torn deliberated for a moment. Which trail should he follow? What was going on?

Looking west, he saw black specks in the sky. Buzzards.

He headed that way.

The buzzards led him to the corpse of another outlaw. The scavengers were already feeding. It wasn't Wheeler. The man had been gutshot. Torn marveled that he had come this far. The other two had taken his horse and guns and boots and even turned his pockets out before riding on.

Finding the dead man did not surprise Torn. He had put the blood and the buzzards together. Since it wasn't Wheeler, he figured he ought to backtrack and trail that lone rider for a spell. He had a hunch that Ash Wheeler hadn't given up, after all. Back there where the four longriders had stopped, Wheeler had probably announced his intention to keep after Chancey Lane. Maybe the others had mutinied. Many of their colleagues had perished simply because Wheeler's ego had been bruised by Chancey's departure. Not that they were the type to mourn fallen comrades. They were just looking out for themselves. They would follow Wheeler and risk their necks for loot, but not for a woman.

If this conjecture was accurate, then the Blue River Gang was finished. The surviving members would scatter to the four winds.

Torn rode back to the spot where the outlaws had split up. He realized that there were at least a dozen other possible explanations for the sign. But he preferred the one he had come up with first, and his following the lone rider north was based on that preference.

When the trail swung east—toward Reddon Springs

and Broken Bow—he felt even better about his judgment call. Surely this had to be Wheeler.

The bastard just wasn't going to give up.

Torn broke off and headed back to the Burkhart place.

He arrived in the middle of the afternoon. Malvern was resting comfortably in the shade. His wound had been dressed. His color was good, his pulse steady. Torn was confident he would mend up nicely.

"Can you travel?" asked Torn.

"Shoot! Give me a few days and I'll be dancin' a do-si-do."

"You try that, you old fool, and I'll kill you," admonished Eliza.

Malvern did not care to be transported in the bed of the wagon with eight dead outlaws, so Torn helped him up into the wagon box. Eliza gathered up the leathers, threading them through her callused fingers. Chancey climbed into the saddle on one of the owlhoot ponies.

"I was wondering if you'd be here when I got back," Torn admitted.

She looked surprised. "You thought I'd run off?"

"Thought you might."

"Maybe you were hoping I would."

"Forget it."

"Look here, Clay Torn," she said hotly. "You just go right ahead and do what you have to do. I won't question it. If I have to go to prison for the crimes I've committed, so be it. But then I'm going to come back here and start all over again, no matter what you do or how long they lock me up. So there."

Torn suppressed a smile as he reined his horse around and steered for the road to Reddon Springs.

CHAPTER 29

ASH WHEELER WAS MAD AS HELL WHEN HE RODE AWAY from the three outlaws who were all that remained of the bunch he had led in pursuit of Judge Torn and Chancey Lane.

Those three had betrayed him. After everything he had done for them. Without him they would still be two-bit cattle rustlers and back-alley bone-breakers. Thanks to the brilliance of his devious criminal mind, they had fared better than any other pack of long-riders.

All this he had taken great pains to point out to them. And still they had refused to follow him to Reddon Springs. Henley had gone so far as to curse him. That was when the ruckus started.

Ash was quite proud of the fact that Henley had gotten the worst of it. Sure, the sonuvabitch had gotten in a few lucky punches. Wheeler's jaw was sore as the dickens, and one of his teeth was aggravatingly loose. But Henley had eaten dust. He had gone down hard, and stayed down, and Wheeler would have drawn his shooting iron and ventilated him just for good measure, except for the expression on Fraser's face. Fraser would have drawn on him. Of this Wheeler was convinced. So Wheeler had refrained from slapping leather. They weren't worth killing, anyway. Cursing them roundly, he had ridden off alone, leaving Fraser and Henley, and the gutshot Lowery, to fend for themselves.

Now, as the long day drew to a close, Ash Wheeler had reached the road into Reddon Springs. Down this he rode, bold as new brass.

He knew Torn was determined to deliver Chancey to Reddon Springs. So Ash had decided to be there waiting for them when they arrived.

But how to get into town unnoticed was a real problem for a man of his notoriety. A couple miles out of town he came across the solution to that problem.

A sodbuster was driving a buckboard into a town, with a pair of mules in the traces. Wheeler rode right on past the man. He kept his chin tucked and fingered the brim of his hat as his horse cantered by. The man in the box was in his twenties, big and strapping, clad in mule-ear boots, stroud trousers, linsey-woolsey shirt, and a flop-brimmed Kossuth hat.

"Howdy!" called the wagoner.

Wheeler said nothing as he pulled on in front of the buckboard. He had seen what he wanted to see. The course of action he had to take clear in his mind, he steered the horse to the side of the ride, reined up, and waited for the wagon to draw abreast of him. Then he fell in alongside, holding his pony to a walk.

"Headed for Reddon Springs?" he asked pleasantly.

"Yep. Going in for supplies. Say, haven't I seen you somewhere before?"

"We've never met. But you've probably seen my picture."

"Your picture?"

"Yeah. On wanted posters. The name's Ash Wheeler."

The recognition—and fear—that flashed across the young man's face was immensely gratifying to Wheeler, whose ego had taken some recent punishment.

He drew his pistol.

"Stop those mules."

The man complied. He was pale as a sheet.

"You . . . you ain't gonna kill me, are you? I ain't got no money. I'm buying on credit at Haskell's shebang. I . . ."

"Shut up and step down."

The man wrapped the leathers around the buckboard's brake bar and stepped down.

"I'm unarmed, mister. And I . . . I got a wife and kid that rely on me. They ain't got nobody else to look after them."

Wheeler heard the panic rising in the man's voice.

"Don't worry," he said amiably. "I'm not going to shoot you down in cold blood. What kind of lies have you heard about me? I'm not a killer, like they want you to believe. It's those banks and stage companies spreading slander about me. I just need to borrow your wagon and your clothes."

"My clothes?"

"Just strip down to your under-riggings, and then you can start walking back to that wife and kid of yours."

The man did as he was told. "Can I keep my boots?"

"Sure you can." Wheeler had already decided that the man's footwear was not the right size anyway. "Now get going. And give my regards to your family."

The man started walking. He threw a few anxious backward glances at Wheeler. Ash waited until he was about fifty paces away. Then he spun his horse around and went after him.

The man yelled and started to run.

Ash waited until he was right up on him before pulling the trigger. The bullet caught the man right between the shoulder blades and slammed him into the dust of the road. Wheeler shot him in the head just to make sure he was dead, before riding back to the wagon.

He took saddlebags and rifle from his rig and let his horse go. Then he stripped down and donned the dead man's clothes. They fit pretty well. And they weren't covered with blood or full of bullet holes, either. Wheeler congratulated himself for having such foresight. Smart, to make the man shed his clothes before gunning him down.

Bundling up his own clothes, Wheeler stashed them under the wagon seat. Here also he concealed the rifle, panniers, and gunbelt with his holstered thumb-buster. Taking up the leathers, he provoked the mules into motion and rolled on toward Reddon Springs, whistling a light-hearted tune.

Close to sundown he arrived in town. No one paid him any special notice. Someone called a greeting from the boardwalk, mistaking him for the man he had recently slain. The Kossuth hat pulled down low to hide his face, Wheeler just waved and kept on going, until he spotted the general store.

As he stopped the wagon in front of the store and jumped down onto the boardwalk, a paunchy man wearing a shopkeeper's apron, with a cigar jutting from his heavily-jowled face stepped through the shebang's doorway.

"Evening, Dave. Coming in a little late aren't you? I was just about to close up and go home to dinner, but I'll . . ."

Moving fast, Wheeler walked right up to the man, planted his revolver in his belly and shoved him backward into the store.

"What the . . . !"

"You'll shut up, is what you'll do," muttered Wheeler.

He threw a quick look around. The walls of the store were lined with shelves laden from floor to rafters. There were two counters, one along the wall to his left, another along the back wall, where a door led to a back alley. It appeared that a person could find just about anything he or she wanted here, from canned goods to calico, ammunition to axs, boots to bridles.

There was only one other person in the store, a boy of about eleven or twelve years of age. He had been sweeping the floor. Now he was rooted to the ground, his eyes as big as saucers as he stared at Wheeler.

"Run for it, Johnny!" cried the shopkeeper.

The boy looked at the back door.

"You move, Johnny, and I'll kill this feller," warned Wheeler. "It'll be your fault he's dead."

The boy didn't move.

"Are you Haskell?" Wheeler asked the man under his gun.

"Yes. What have you done to Dave Ludlow?"

"Don't worry about him. Worry about yourself and how you're going to stay alive."

"I know you. Aren't you . . . ?"

Wheeler smiled. "That's right. So you better do what I tell you."

"What do you want?"

"I want what belongs to me."

"I don't understand."

"You will. Hey, boy."

"Yessir?"

"Can you find the local sheriff?"

"I guess so. Sure."

"Then find him. Tell him to come to the middle of the street in front of this store. Unarmed. I want to talk to him. The name's Ash Wheeler."

"Jeepers!" breathed the youngster.

"Tell him that if he tries anything foolish, like busting in here slinging lead, I'll make dead certain Mr. Haskell here meets his maker. Got that?"

"Yessir."

"Good boy. But first, go to the wagon and bring me that rifle and those saddlebags under the seat."

The boy did as he was told. He didn't even consider turning the rifle on Ash Wheeler. Wheeler had known he wouldn't.

"Thanks, son. Now move that wagon out of the way, and go tell the local badgetoter what I said."

The boy took off.

"Mr. Haskell, I'd like to see some of your best hard twist."

"Rope? What for?"

"To tie you up. I'll try to make you as comfortable as possible, though, seein' as how we're going to be here a while, you and me."

CHAPTER 30

BILLY STEPTOE WAS THE DEPUTY SHERIFF OF REDDON Springs. The boy named Johnny found him having his dinner at the usual hour in the Prairie Cafe. Steptoe sat at a table by the window, moodily picking at his food, looking out at the darkening street, and wondering what the heck had happened to Sheriff Ben Rawlins.

Rawlins had assured his deputy that he would be back yesterday, if not sooner. He had seemed to be in a mighty big hurry to ride out after receiving that telegram. Steptoe had not been made privy to the wire's contents, but yesterday he had dropped by the telegraph office and asked the operator if he remembered anything at all about the message.

"Ben told me not to tell anybody about it," said the

telegrapher, an irascible, scrawny, chicken-necked character named Ferrin. "So scat."

Steptoe had bristled at the disrespect in Ferrin's voice and demeanor. Didn't the idiot see the badge on his shirt? Wasn't that tin star supposed to mean something?

"Look here," said Steptoe, trying his best to sound sternly officious. "This is sheriff business. Ben's overdue. He could be in trouble."

Ferrin scoffed at that notion. "Ben Rawlins can take care of himself." He gave the lanky, boyish-looking deputy a skeptical once-over that said, louder than words, *which is more than I could say for you.*

Steptoe tried not to get aggravated. He reminded himself that Ferrin was an old curmudgeon whose only pleasure in life came from making other people miserable. So he ought not to take what the crotchety old fool said seriously.

"Ferrin," said Steptoe coldly. "If Ben's in trouble, and he finds out you wouldn't tell me what I need to know, he might not be too happy with you."

The telegrapher leaned back in his chair, adopting a deliberately insouciant pose, and sneered.

"Oh, I forgot. You're the big augur around these parts now, aren't you? That's just hard for me to remember. Why, it seems like only yesterday that you were a barefoot, freckle-faced, snot-nosed kid who used to run messages for me."

"Just tell me about the telegram."

"Won't be any help to you. All it said was something about a judge coming here to Reddon Springs with . . . I think the initials were CL. Said for Ben to meet up with them."

"Who was it from?"

Ferrin shook his head. "Had another initial at the end. Can't remember what it was."

"Well, then, where did the wire come from?"

"The line to Lonesome Pine."

"A judge?" puzzled Steptoe, rubbing his chin. "Wonder what it all means?"

Ferrin shrugged. "Beats me?" His key started to clatter with the signature of another telegrapher prefacing an incoming message.

Steptoe had left it at that, knowing he could get nothing more out of Ferrin.

So now, the next day, he was starting to worry. Not so much about Ben Rawlins—truth be known, he wouldn't go so far as to call Rawlins anything close to a friend—but about all the responsibility that had been dumped on his unprepared shoulders.

Rawlins had given him the deputy's star as a favor to his father, a local rancher, and one of Ben's drinking buddies. Billy had never fired his charcoal-burner in anger. He was here wearing this tin because he had absolutely no desire to be a cowpuncher. But he had never counted on this: being in charge of keeping the peace in Reddon Springs. He had spent a lot of time recently praying that nobody started any trouble.

When he saw Johnny coming through the door at a dead run—and read the look of alarm on the boy's face—Billy Steptoe had a hunch all his prayers had been for naught, and his stomach began to perform slow rolls.

"Billy!" yelped Johnny as he sprinted through the half-filled chop house to the deputy's table. "Billy, there's . . ."

"Hush!" said Steptoe fiercely, uncomfortably conscious of the fact that all eyes in the room were turned on him and the boy. "We don't want the whole town to know."

Johnny stared, stupefied. "Huh?" He wondered how Billy Steptoe could possibly know that the notorious Ash Wheeler was in town and holding a gun to Mr. Haskell's head.

"Just tell me, real quiet-like," said Steptoe.

When Johnny told him, the color drained from Billy Steptoe's youthful face. Aware that most of the eatery's patrons were still watching him, wondering what had happened, Steptoe tried to regain his composure.

"Johnny, sit down and I'll order you a sarsparilla."

"But . . . but . . ."

"Sit down, Johnny!" hissed Steptoe.

The boy obeyed. Steptoe got the waiter's attention, and ordered Johnny's drink. Then he forced himself to finish his dinner in as leisurely a manner as possible—and amazed himself with this exhibition of monumental self-discipline.

Billy Steptoe was going to find out a lot more about himself in the next few hours.

It was dark when Billy Steptoe appeared in the street in front of Haskell's general store. The town was quiet. Most folks were at the dinner table. The businesses along Front Street were closed up, except for Cheyenne Charlie's Saloon down at the other end of town. From there came the faint sound of the notoriously out-of-tune piano. A dog barked in the alley behind the she-bang, which looked to Billy to be as closed-up and peaceful as everything else. No light inside. The front door shut. He ventured closer, to the edge of the boardwalk, wondering if this was some horrible practical joke being played on him. He knew the town at large didn't have much respect for him, at least as a deputy sheriff, and he didn't really blame them. What had he done to earn their respect? Hauled a few drunken cowpokes to jail? It wasn't the badge that won confidence, it was the man behind the badge.

"That's close enough," came a voice from the dark innards of Haskell's store.

Steptoe jumped at the voice. Closer now, he could tell the door was ever-so-slightly ajar.

"What do you want?" asked Billy, and was mighty relieved when his voice didn't crack.

"I want you to do exactly what I say. If you don't, you'll be short one storekeeper."

"Are you really Ash Wheeler?"

"The one and only."

Billy Steptoe felt the blood freeze in his veins. He felt the urgent need to sit down. The tin star on his shirt felt very heavy all of a sudden.

"What do you want me to do?"

"There'll be a feller through here, maybe tonight, maybe tomorrow. Name of Clay Torn. He's a federal judge."

Billy Steptoe's mind flew back to what the telegrapher had said.

A judge coming here to Reddon Springs . . .

"He's got a woman with him. Say, you don't look too good."

"I'm . . . fine," said Steptoe lamely.

"Why, you're just a wet-behind-the-ears kid, aren't you, deputy? Wonder how come Ben Rawlins hired the likes of you?"

"You know Ben?"

"Never mind. You scared, deputy?"

"Some."

"Good. You oughta be. Now, when this Judge Torn rides in here he'll look you up, since you're the law. That's when you tell him to bring Chancey here to me, pronto."

"Chancey? Chancey Lane?"

A judge coming here to Reddon Springs with . . . I think the initials were CL.

The Lady Outlaw herself!

Billy Steptoe had the feeling he was in way over his head. Punching cows was looking a whole lot better.

"You got that, deputy?"

"Yeah. I've got it."

"Tell Judge Torn I'll kill Haskell if he doesn't do what I say."

"Okay."

"And I wouldn't go spreading this around, deputy, if I was you. I reckon if the word gets out that I'm here there'll be some brass-plated fools who go to thinking about that big reward they could collect, and then they might try something stupid, and then you'll have a lot of dead pilgrims to plant."

Steptoe nodded. "I see what you mean."

"Good. Now go on."

Steptoe walked away. He got as far as the next alley, into which he stumbled. Doubled over, he threw up the entire dinner he had gone to such great pains to eat.

When he straightened up he nearly jumped out of his skin.

A tall man in black stood there in front of him.

"Are you going to live?" asked Torn.

"Who are you?"

"Clay Torn. Federal judge. Was that Ash Wheeler you were talking to."

"Yeah. He's holed up in the general store."

"There's somebody in there with him?"

"Yeah. Joe Haskell. He owns the store. Wheeler wants you to . . ."

"I know what he wants," said Torn grimly. "And he's going to learn that you don't always get what you want in this world."

CHAPTER 31

WHEN BILLY STEPTOE ACCOMPANIED CLAY TORN INTO the sheriff's office, he found three people waiting there. Malvern Burkhart was stretched out on the bunk in an empty cell. Eliza sat in a chair beside him, holding his hand. And Chancey Lane stood at a window, where she had been watching the street with a rifle in her hands.

Steptoe stared at Chancey. He didn't require an introduction to know that this was the infamous Lady Outlaw of bawdy ballad and dime-novel fame, in the flesh.

"Wheeler's here," Torn told Chancey.

"You were right."

Torn nodded.

"You knew he'd be here?" queried Steptoe.

"Yes. We followed a trail of bodies. Well, one at

least. Few miles out of town. I don't know who he is, but I'm sure Wheeler shot him down. That's why we waited until dark to come in. Does anybody else in town know what's going on?"

"No, I don't think so."

"Good. Let's try to keep it that way. Enough people have been killed."

"Joe Haskell's going to get killed if you don't do what Wheeler wants."

"It's not going to happen that way."

Steptoe rubbed his eyes. "I wish Sheriff Rawlins was here," he admitted. "I never counted on anything like this."

"When you put on that badge you should have," said Torn sternly. "As for Rawlins, he's dead."

"Dead? How do you know?"

"We killed him."

Steptoe was struck speechless.

"Rawlins was crooked," continued Torn. "He was in Ash Wheeler's back pocket."

"That can't be."

"It's true," said Chancey. "I know. Ash told me. Rawlins helped him pull a robbery and got a share of the loot for his trouble."

Steptoe looked at her, Torn, and finally at the badge pinned to his shirt.

Then he pulled the tin star loose and tossed it on the spur-scarred kneehole desk in one corner of the office.

"I'm going back to being a cowboy."

Torn retrieved the badge and tossed it right back to Steptoe.

"Not tonight you're not."

"I'm not cut out for this."

"Too bad. I need your help to get Ash Wheeler."

"How?"

"Is there a back way into that store?"

"Well, yes, but I reckon it's bolted shut."

"I'm sure it is. Now listen close. This is what we're going to do . . ."

An hour later Torn walked up to the front of the general store with Chancey Lane and called out to Ash Wheeler.

"Hey, Wheeler! You wanted to see us?"

The door was yanked open. It was pitch black inside the store. Try as he might, Torn could see absolutely nothing beyond the threshold.

"Are you heeled, Judge?"

Torn held open his frock coat. Even in the darkness, this close, Wheeler could see that his gunbelt was gone. But the outlaw wasn't going to take any chances.

"Take off your coat and turn around slowly."

Torn did as he was told. Satisfied that Torn was unarmed, Wheeler told them to come inside. "Ladies first," he sneered.

Chancey hesitated and glanced at Torn, and he could see the fear in her eyes. Ironically, it was fear for his well-being, not her own, even though Torn figured there was a better than fifty-fifty chance that Wheeler was going to kill her, too.

He nodded, and she stepped into the store.

Wheeler grabbed her as soon as she was across the threshold and swung her against one of the counters. As Torn came through the door, Wheeler jerked the black frock coat out of his hand, kicked the door shut, and put his gun to Torn's head. He thumbed the hammer back. The double click of the revolver's action was very loud in Torn's ear.

"You've caused me a lot of trouble, you bastard," snarled the outlaw.

"Glad to hear it."

Wheeler pistol-whipped him. Torn was half-expecting something along those lines, so he tried to duck. The gun barrel caught him a glancing blow. Bright lights dancing in his squeezed-shut eyes, Torn fell to his hands and knees, dazed, nauseated.

"Don't!" cried Chancey.

"Shut up!" yelled Wheeler, infuriated. "You slut. I guess you laid with him, too, didn't you? Like you did with everybody in the gang. *Didn't you?*"

Chancey's reply was coldly and flatly delivered. "No, I did not. But I wanted to."

"Well, he's going to be dead in about one minute, so you're just out of luck."

Torn got slowly to his feet. "Where's Haskell?"

"I'm here," said the storekeeper from somewhere near the back of the store.

"Are you okay?"

"Well, I'm tied up like a turkey on Thanksgiving. And I'm hungry as all get-out, since I had to miss my dinner to play host to Mr. Wheeler."

Torn smiled faintly. Storekeeper Haskell was long on nerve.

"You'll never get out of this town alive, Wheeler," he said.

"Oh, I reckon I could if I wanted. But I don't aim to try."

"What do you mean?"

"I mean Chancey and me are gonna go down in a blaze of glory, Judge."

Torn experienced an unpleasant sinking feeling in the pit of his stomach.

"You're as crazy as they say."

Wheeler chuckled. "Who wants to live forever."

"I don't want to die," said Chancey.

"Well, you're gonna, because I'm gonna to die, and you're going with me. It's clear I can't trust you, so I'm sure as hell not gonna leave you behind."

Torn fought down the panic rising within him. Stay calm and keep thinking, those were the keys to survival. *And where the hell was that deputy?*

"Soon as I blow a hole through the judge here," gloated Wheeler, "you and me are gonna shoot up this town. Gonna get these good folks all stirred up. And they'll have to gun us down in the street. We'll die famous, Chancey. And we'll die together. They'll write books about us."

"I'm not going anywhere with you anymore, Ash Wheeler," snapped Chancey. "Least of all to the grave."

There came three loud taps on the back door.

"What the hell is that?" asked Wheeler.

"Haskell, get away from that door!" yelled Torn as he threw himself on the floor.

Wheeler got off one shot at Torn—and missed— before the back door disintegrated in an explosion that rocked the whole building. Merchandise came tumbling down from the shelves. Burning wood shrapnel filled the air. The front windows shattered. The explosion was deafening. A stack of blankets caught fire, illuminated the wrecked interior of the store. Torn saw Wheeler on the ground. The blast had knocked him off his feet. Torn looked for Chancey through the acrid smoke. She was on the ground across the room, lifting her dress to get to the saber-knife tied with hobble strings to her calf.

She's taking too long, thought Torn.

Ash was getting to his feet. He still had his gun. Torn gathered himself up and ran right at the outlaw, hitting him low, driving him back against the wall. Wheeler's gun went off. The bullet drilled the counter inches away from Chancey. Torn hit Wheeler's gun arm with such a blow that he knocked the pistol loose. As the gun clattered on the floor, Wheeler punched him solidly in the face. Torn sprawled backward. Wheeler pulled a double-bladed ax from a barrel and raised it high overhead, to bring it down with a savage shriek. Torn rolled and the ax bit deep into the floor.

"Chancey!" yelled Torn.

She threw him the saber-knife. He bounced to his feet and ducked under the ax swung laterally at shoulder level.

For an instant, as the weight of the ax took him a little off balance, Wheeler was open to attack.

Torn slipped in and cut him open with the saber-knife.

Wheeler fell to his knees, trying to hold himself together, his arms tightly wrapped around his midsection. He stared at the blood pooling on the floor beneath him. Then he looked across the room at Chancey and reached out for her with one clawing, blood-stained hand, before he breathed his last and pitched forward on his face.

Billy Steptoe came through the ragged smoldering hole in the back wall. He spared Wheeler the merest glance before going to Haskell. The rope-bound storekeeper was rolled up in a tight ball, half-buried beneath busted sacks of flour and brown sugar.

"Joe, are you hurt?"

"Jesus, Billy! What did you use on my back door?"

"A keg of black powder. I got it from Murphy's mercantile."

"You used powder from my competition's stock to blow up my store?" Haskell started laughing like a loon.

Billy Steptoe grinned and proceeded to untie him.

Torn walked over to Chancey and gave her a hand up. She tried not to look at the bloody saber-knife in his hand.

"You better go to the Burkharts," he said. "They'll be worried sick about you."

She nodded, squeezed his hand and, stepping over Wheeler's corpse, ran out into the night.

Having found the storekeeper, who immediately set about extinguishing the several small fires in the wreckage, Billy Steptoe crossed the room to Torn.

"Aren't you afraid she'll get away?" asked the deputy.

"Who?"

"Chancey Lane. Now that Ash Wheeler's dead, I reckon she's the most wanted outlaw in the territory."

"Chancey Lane's dead, too."

"Huh?"

"She died here tonight. You're going to be my witness to that, deputy."

"I am?"

Torn smiled. "Listen close. This is what we're going to do . . ."

Billy Steptoe sighed.

Saddle-up to these

THE REGULATOR by *Dale Colter*
Sam Slater, blood brother of the Apache and a cunning bounty-hunter, is out to collect the big price on the heads of the murderous Pauley gang. He'll give them a single choice: surrender and live, or go for your sixgun.

THE REGULATOR—Diablo At Daybreak by *Dale Colter*
The Governor wants the blood of the Apache murderers who ravaged his daughter. He gives Sam Slater a choice: work for him, or face a noose. Now Slater must hunt down the deadly renegade Chacon…Slater's Apache brother.

THE JUDGE by *Hank Edwards*
Federal Judge Clay Torn is more than a judge—sometimes he has to be the jury *and* the executioner. Torn pits himself against the most violent and ruthless man in Kansas, a battle whose final verdict will judge one man right…and one man dead.

THE JUDGE—War Clouds by *Hank Edwards*
Judge Clay Torn rides into Dakota where the Cheyenne are painting for war and the army is shining steel and loading lead. If war breaks out, someone is going to make a pile of money on a river of blood.